# "What is this, an inquistition?"

Jared's question demanded an answer. "You know all about me," Alice replied. "Why shouldn't I find out something about you?"

"I don't know everything about you," Jared said with a wry smile. "I don't know how many boyfriends you've had since I was there. You said you'd been in love too many times to mention. Are you really so fickle? Was I just one of many?" he said, his eyes hardening.

"Would it matter if you were?" she retorted.

"I don't like to think of you offering yourself to every Tom, Dick and Harry who shows interest."

"You think that's what I do?" she said sharply.

"Well," he said coldly. "You certainly wanted me then—if you'll remember you virtually threw yourself at me."

**Margaret Mayo** began writing quite by chance when the engineering company she worked for wasn't very busy and she found herself with time on her hands. Today, with more than thirty romance novels to her credit, she admits that writing governs her life to a large extent. When she and her husband holiday—Cornwall is their favorite spot—Margaret always has a notebook and camera on hand and is constantly looking for fresh ideas. She lives in the countryside near Stafford, England.

## Books by Margaret Mayo

### HARLEQUIN ROMANCE

2439—A TASTE OF PARADISE
2474—DIVIDED LOYALTIES
2557—DANGEROUS JOURNEY
2602—RETURN A STRANGER
2795—IMPULSIVE CHALLENGE
2805—AT DAGGERS DRAWN
2937—FEELINGS

### HARLEQUIN PRESENTS

963—PASSIONATE VENGEANCE
1045—SAVAGE AFFAIR
1108—A PAINFUL LOVING

# Unexpected Inheritance

## Margaret Mayo

# Harlequin Books

**TORONTO • NEW YORK • LONDON**
**AMSTERDAM • PARIS • SYDNEY • HAMBURG**
**STOCKHOLM • ATHENS • TOKYO • MILAN**

Original hardcover edition published in 1988
by Mills & Boon Limited

ISBN 0-373-02955-1

Harlequin Romance first edition January 1989

# CHAPTER ONE

EXCITEMENT surged through Alice as the plane lost height and St Lucia loomed nearer and nearer. This was the first time she had ever flown, the first time she had left England, and had it not been against regulations she would have raced down the aisle, looking through each of the windows in turn trying to find the best view.

She felt like a child again, instead of twenty-two, and her blue eyes were huge and wide and full of wonder. 'Look,' she cried, shaking Tony's arm, 'look at the sea, look at those blues and greens, aren't they out of this world? It's almost transparent, I can actually see the bottom. Oh, Tony, I'm so glad you talked me into coming!

'I can't wait to swim in that water,' she went on, giving a delicious shudder of anticipation. 'I bet it's warm and silky and absolute heaven!'

The island was coming up to meet them at an alarming speed now, and she put her hands on the arms of her seat, tensing her body slightly, her eyes shining. This was a whole new experience—and she loved it.

They touched down with scarcely a bump and she could not wait for the plane to come to a halt. She wanted to scramble off and run and shout and jump for joy. She had never realised her grandfather lived in such a breathtaking part of the world. Oh, Mum, she said silently, what a lot you missed out on!

The air was warm but not stifling, and Alice turned her face up to the sun, feeling it caress her skin, feeling

5

too a sudden lightening of her mind, a lifting of some of the sadness and heartache that had dogged her last months. Everything was going to be all right.

Tony ran a forefinger down her arched throat. 'Come on, we still have another plane to catch. You'll have plenty of time for sun-worshipping later.'

She wrinkled her nose. 'It's all right for you, you've been abroad before. I can't get over how warm and clean and fresh everywhere is. It's fantastic—it's like paradise!'

'And how would you know?' Tony jeered, his brown eyes alight with good humour.

She tossed back her mane of blonde hair. 'This is my idea of paradise and I don't care what you say.'

He smiled indulgently. 'You're a pretty terrific girl, Alice Alexander—have I told you that before?'

'Actually, no,' she replied airily, 'but you don't have to, I already know.' And with a mischievous laugh she skipped on ahead of him, feeling only slightly troubled. She hoped Tony wasn't getting too serious. He was a fun companion and she liked him a lot, but her feelings went no deeper. He had been there when she needed someone, and for that she would be eternally grateful.

The smaller plane was yet another experience. It was nothing like the jet which had travelled so smoothly that she had scarcely known they were flying. Now they were buffeted by the air currents and they flew so much lower that she could see the vegetation on the islands, and the silver beaches, and the brilliant sails of the boats. Her face was glowing and her eyes shining, and she could never remember feeling so excited.

When they finally touched down on Perle Island the promised car was waiting. The black driver greeted them with a toothpaste-white grin, though he looked unsure when he discovered Alice was not alone.

'He's my friend,' she explained. 'It'll be all right.'

Whether he understood she was not sure, because his English was so heavily accented by local dialect that it was impossible to understand him. Nevertheless he quite happily stowed their cases, but when Alice made to scramble into the front seat beside him, wanting to have a clear view of the island as they drove, Tony would not let her. 'I want you with me,' he said. 'I want to see your face, you pull some delightful expressions.'

She bobbed her tongue out and then sat on the edge of her seat, winding down her window, exclaiming time and time again as something new and exciting took her eye.

What a fantastic island it was! Everywhere was lush and green. Some of the trees were covered in a blaze of red flowers, and she caught glimpses of banana plantations and orange groves; it was all so different and exotic that she could not sit still. There were magnificent houses tucked away in corners, and each time they approached one she wondered whether it was Blue Vista.

Then they began to climb, higher and higher, and she caught only glimpses of the sea now through the foliage of amazing trees and the sloping trunks of palms that grew at all sorts of drunken angles. Brilliantly plumaged birds flew in their path and the breeze in her face was soft and fragrant. It was a totally different world.

'Well, Alice,' said Tony, when they finally approached a huge stone house set into the side of the mountain, 'this really is something. I guess your grandfather must have been a rich old guy to own a place like this.'

'And we never saw a penny,' she said quietly, a sudden shadow dulling her eyes.

'You had a rotten deal,' he admitted, 'but it looks as if it's all coming to you now. You're going to be one hell of a rich girl.'

'Riches won't bring my mother back,' she protested.

He nodded understandingly and pulled her to him. Alice

pressed her head into his shoulder. Tony really was a comfort. He wasn't handsome or macho or anything like that; he was a year older than herself and was ordinary, and he had black curly hair and a funny crooked smile and she liked him a lot. 'Don't be sad, Alice,' he said. 'Just imagine what a difference this is going to make to your life.'

'He hated us,' she muttered. 'He never once got in touch. Can you believe that? He's never even seen me. And now this. I wish I hadn't come. He can keep his rotten money, I don't want any of it. I hate his guts as much as he hated ours!'

'It's your right,' said Tony firmly. 'You're his only living relative, isn't that so?'

She nodded.

'Well then, stop being morbid. Think what you can do with his money instead. Think what a difference it'll make. Oh, my lovely silly girl, I adore you!'

He kissed her hard and held her tight, and Alice groaned inwardly. He sounded suddenly serious, and she could do without such complications. Nevertheless, she was glad he had come with her. She could never have faced this alone. In fact she probably would not have come if it hadn't been for Tony's insistence. She owed it to herself, he kept telling her, until in the end she believed him.

When the letter had arrived a few weeks ago from her grandfather's solicitor she had thought it was in response to her own news that her mother had died following a sudden severe and inexplicable brain haemorrhage. Her mother had always said that if anything ever happened to her Alice was not to tell her grandfather, but despite Alice's bitterness and resentment towards him, something moral deep down inside her insisted that she let him know.

But instead the letter from Mr Lewis was to inform her that her grandfather had died too, shortly after receiving the news of his daughter's death, and she was requested to fly out to the West Indies for a meeting with Mr Lewis. He did not say why he wanted to see her, and she could only assume it was because she had inherited something in her grandfather's will.

An air ticket and a cheque to cover her immediate expenses were enclosed. At St Lucia she was to transfer to a light aircraft, and when she landed on Perle Island a car would meet her and take her to Blue Vista, which she knew was her grandfather's house. It had all been very unexpected, and her initial reaction had been one of consuming anger.

'Why the hell should I?' she had remarked angrily to Tony after showing him the letter. Tony lived next door and was more like a brother than anything else. They had never dated, he had his girlfriends and she her boyfriends, but she did not know what she would have done without him and his parents during the dark days after her mother death.

'And why shouldn't you?' he said. 'It's pretty obvious you're going to benefit in some way, otherwise you wouldn't be asked to go out there. Who knows, perhaps the old guy's left you everthing. It was your mother he fell out with, not you.'

'But he's never shown any interest in me.'

Tony shrugged. 'Who else could he leave his money to?'

'I don't know,' said Alice. 'It's a mystery to me. He must have friends out there, though, people he's grown close to. He left England twenty years ago.'

'Whatever the case, it's obvious he's put his family first,' said Tony firmly. 'If I were in your shoes, Alice, I wouldn't hesitate. My goodness me, if he wants you to have his money then don't let pride sit in your way!

And he had gone on and on in the same vein until finally Alice had given in. 'I'll come with you,' he said, 'if you'd like me to? I can easily take a couple of weeks' holiday.'

'Oh, Tony, would you?' Alice was relieved. As she had never travelled any great distance on her own, the thought of the long journey was daunting to say the least.

'For you, Alice, anything,' he smiled.

Then her brow creased. 'It might cost you a lot of money.'

He shrugged. 'So would any holiday. I'd like to come Alice—I really would.' And so their plans had been made.

The car came to a halt outside the house and Alice pushed her thoughts to one side. The smile was back on her lips as she jumped out. 'Come on, slowcoach,' she called over her shoulder, 'let's find out what this is all about!'

They followed the chauffeur to an open door at the side of the stone house and Alice did not have time to take very much in. But she was aware of the overall beauty of the place, and found it cool and welcoming after their long journey.

The man left their cases at the bottom of a flight of stairs and continued into the house. He tapped on a door and pushed it open, and Alice saw a room where the blinds were drawn against the sunlight. He said something completely unintelligible, indicated that they should go in, then left.

It was difficult to see at first, after the brightness from outside, but Alice could make out a man's shape near the window. 'Mr Lewis?' She peered through the gloom.

'Who is that with you?' The man's tone was clipped, the question completely unexpected.

'Tony Chatwin, a friend of mine,' she said, frowning.

'You were supposed to come alone.'

Alice lifted her chin, taking an instant dislike to this man who was handling her late grandfather's affairs. She sought Tony's hand. 'Is it a crime to want company on such a long trip? You said nothing about me travelling by myself.'

'It was presumed.'

She saw the man's arm go out and with one swift sharp action the blind shot up and sunlight streamed into the room. For the first time Alice saw his face clearly, and the shock was like a blow to her solar plexus. Apart from a few lines around his eyes and mouth that had not been there six years ago he looked no different. 'I don't believe it!' she gasped. She did not want to believe it. Please God, it was not him. She clapped her hands to her cheeks and stared open-mouthed.

He was a tall muscular man with sunny blond hair and a tremendous all-year-round tan. He was somewhere in his mid-thirties and had piercing blue eyes and a smile that made one feel special, except that at this moment he was not smiling. But Alice had once felt the effect of it and had succumbed, and then been forced to nurse her wounds for a long time afterwards. He was wearing white shorts and a blue summer shirt and his arms and his legs were as deeply tanned as his face.

Tony looked at her and frowned. 'You know this man?'

Dumbly she nodded. Did she know this man? That was the understatement of the year! She knew him too well, and she had never wanted to see him again.

'You're not Mr Lewis!' she accused shrilly.

'I didn't say I was.'

'So what the hell are you doing here?'

'I live here,' he answered calmly.

Alice shook her head. How could he live here when this was her grandfather's house? It was all too much to take in. 'I'm confused,' she said, turning to Tony.

'Just who is this guy?' he asked, drawing her to him, sensing her hostility, but not understanding it.

'Someone my mother met a few years ago.'

Tony looked at the man who was a head taller than

himself. 'Perhaps, sir, you'd kindly tell me what your name is and what you're doing here? Whoever you are I can see you're upsetting Alice, and I don't like it.'

Tony looked very young and inadequate against this other tougher, more physical man, but his chin jutted and his eyes were hard, and his arm was still protectively around Alice. She felt proud of him.

'I don't owe you an explanation.' Blue eyes met brown with cold dislike. 'Alice knows who I am. If she has any questions she can put them to me herself.'

Alice drew in a deep unsteady breath. 'His name is Jared Duvall,' she said in a swift undertone to Tony, trying to smile but failing, her eyes flashing as she glared at her antagonist. 'OK, Jared, so what's this all about? Where's Mr Lewis? And what are you doing in my grandfather's house? No——' She stopped abruptly, wrenching free from Tony and striding towards the older man. 'Don't tell me, I think I know.' The truth suddenly hit her like a ton of hot bricks. 'You're a friend of my grandfather, aren't you? He sent you to spy on us. It was no coincidence you meeting my mother; you knew all along who she was, and all about us.'

Less than a foot separated them now and Alice was fuming. Her legs were astride, her arms akimbo, her whole stance full of aggression.

His eyes were a darker blue than her own, the whites very clear, his lashes quite brown considering how fair his hair was. He was the sort of man who would turn any woman's head. His features weren't perfect; his nose looked as though it had once been broken, his mouth was wide, and his jaw square with a cleft in it. Nevertheless he was a very sensuous man with a charisma that could not be denied, and the first time Alice saw him she had been bowled over.

Her head was thrust back as she scowled fiercely. His

lips quirked, as though her angry words amused him. 'I can't deny it. It's all true.'

'But why?' she demanded. 'Why did my grandfather wait sixteen years? And even then he hadn't the guts to come and see us himself, he had to send his *henchman.*' Her lip curled as she spat the word, trying to make it clear exactly what she thought of him. 'He needn't have bothered.'

'Daniel was ill,' said Jared quietly.

'And he decided that that was the right time to find out how his daughter and her illegitimate child were doing? His conscience was bothering him, was it? He thought he hadn't long to live and he'd best make amends? God, I feel sick! All those years my mother struggled . . . I hate my grandfather, I've hated him ever since I was old enough to understand what he did to my mother, and I hate you for doing his dirty work for him!'

Jared's lips firmed. 'Your mother had an equal opportunity to contact Daniel.'

'He threw her out,' cried Alice. 'You know that. He disowned her completely. "No child of mine is bringing a bastard into his house," that's what he told her.'

'It was an understandable reaction,' said Jared evenly. 'But he calmed down eventually.'

'Oh, yes, that's why he left England and came to live here. Hell, Jared, don't make excuses for the man! I know what he was like—my mother's told me about him often enough. God, he was so strict with her it's unbelievable! She wasn't allowed to do anything, not have a boyfriend, not go out to dances, nothing.'

'He was old-fashioned, I admit,' nodded Jared, 'but he loved her dearly. He was trying to protect her. When your grandmother left him your mother was only twelve. He was absolutely stricken.'

'Of course,' she said scathingly. 'I've heard all about

that. He wouldn't let her take her daughter, but instead of giving his child the love and affection she needed he made her life hell. What a swine of a man he was! I can understand why my grandmother deserted him. What I can't understand is why she married him in the first place. How could anyone love a man like that? If you ask me, he was born in the wrong era.'

Jared's face had remained expressionless during her outburst. Now he said quietly, 'Over the years Daniel began to wish he hadn't been quite so hard.'

Alice's head jerked. 'He still didn't attempt to get in touch with her.'

Something flickered in his eyes. 'Your mother made no attempt to get in touch with him. Don't ever forget that.'

'He sent you instead,' she flung dismissively, her eyes full of pain and anger. 'What I want to know is why you didn't say who you were. If my mother had known her father was trying to get in touch the rift might have been healed before she died.'

'You really think that?'

'Yes. Yes, I do.'

'I'll tell you something, shall I, Alice, something your mother should have told you.'

'What?' she snapped rudely, unable to think of anything that he knew about her mother and she didn't.

'Your mother knew your grandfather had sent me.'

Alice's eyes widened. 'I don't believe you. Why didn't she tell me? Why didn't you tell me? You're lying!'

'Gilian thought you might try and persuade her to see him.'

'Why would I do that?' demanded Alice. 'I hate him! I hate everything he's done to her.'

'But there have been occasions when you've questioned your mother about him, when you've let her see how much you miss having a family.'

Alice shrugged. 'So what? They were minor lapses. I'd never, ever have agreed to her coming out here.'

'No?' Jared's brows lifted. 'I think if I'd asked you, you would have done, and your mother knew that. We had a lot of discussions. I did my utmost to persuade her, but she was very bitter and very stubborn. I think the years served to increase her rancour rather than diminish it.'

Alice was furious that she had not been told the real reason for Jared's visit, that they had both let her think their meeting was accidental. 'I'm glad she refused you,' she grated through her teeth. 'And I'd have backed her every inch of the way.' She refused to think otherwise. 'Suppose you tell me exactly what you're doing here. Did you live with my grandfather?'

Jared nodded.

And he thought he was going to take over the house! She would see about that. She compressed her lips and swung away, and saw Tony. Poor Tony; she had forgotten he was there.

'Sorry about all that,' she said quietly. 'I had no idea any of this was going to happen, none at all.' And by the look on his face Tony had no idea what was going on either.

'When am I going to see Mr Lewis?' Alice turned once again to Jared.

'In the morning.'

She frowned. 'Why not now?'

'Because he's busy, and he thought you'd want to rest after your journey.'

Rest—after coming all this way to find out what her grandfather had left her in his will? That was the last thing on her mind. She wanted to know, and she wanted to know now.

'Perhaps you can tell me what it's all about?' she demanded. 'It's a heck of a way to come to hear a will read out. Why couldn't I have been told by letter?'

'Because it was your grandfather's wish,' he said smoothly, 'and I'm afraid you'll have to wait. It's nothing to do with me, it's a family matter.'

'That's right, it is private,' she thrust, 'but you seem to be doing your best to shove your nose in all the same.'

His eyes hardened. 'Your grandfather and I were very close. It was his idea that I went to England.'

'And was it his idea that you live here?'

Jared drew a breath before saying quietly, 'You'll find out, in good time. Perhaps you'd like to freshen up?'

He led the way from the room without even looking at Tony, and Alice was furious. She caught hold of Tony's hand and hurried after Jared. 'How dare you ignore my friend!'

'I'm sorry,' Jared at last looked at the boy, 'but the idea was for Alice to come alone.'

Tony eyed him boldly. 'She didn't relish the long journey by herself.'

'And you decided to accompany her? How gallant! What are you after?'

'Jared!' Alice was horrified.

He smiled blandly. 'Do forgive me, I have a naturally suspicious mind.'

But his apology meant nothing, he was quite serious.

'Please follow,' he continued glibly. 'I'm sure there's a room somewhere you can use.'

Jared picked up one suitcase and Tony the other and they filed up the stairs. Alice was still fuming. He was as hateful as that day six years ago when he had brutally told her she was young and foolish and had a lot of growing up to do.

Well, she was grown up now all right, and she had no intention of letting him put her down again. He seemed to think he was in charge, but this was her grandfather's house, and she had as much right here as anyone; if she wanted to bring a friend then there was nothing he could do about it.

She touched Tony's arm and he turned, and she smiled encouragingly. He gave an expressive shrug and carried on up.

'Jared stopped at the first door he came to and thrust it open. He looked directly at the younger man. 'You can have this room.' Then he continued on along the corridor.

'I'll see you later,' said Alice sympathetically, and then reluctantly followed Jared. He turned a couple of corners and walked right to the far end of a long corridor before finally pushing open another door.

Alice could not contain herself. This was ridiculous! 'What are you trying to do?' she demanded. 'Make sure we don't creep into each other's rooms in the middle of the night? There's no need. We don't have that sort of a relationship.'

Jared's thick brows rose. 'You expect me to believe that? You're forgetting I know what a passionate little creature you are.'

Alice felt the blood rush to her cheeks. 'That was a mistake,' she snapped. 'I learned my lesson.'

His mouth twisted wryly. 'I'm pleased to hear it.' He stood her case at the bottom of the bed. 'The bathroom's through there. I'll organise some tea for when you come down.'

She was about to tell him not to bother when she realised Tony would probably welcome a drink. 'Thank you, that would be nice.'

Their eyes met and there was a sudden unfathomable expression in his depths. Jared covered the few feet between them in less time than it took her to draw breath, and Alice's heart began to thump as his intention became clear.

She backed a pace and put out her hands to protect herself, but he took them in his own, pulling them behind him and then sliding his arms around her back and fiercely claiming her mouth with his.

It all happened in a matter of seconds, and the pleasure his kiss created was sheer insanity. The years that had passed had done nothing to lessen the effect he had on her. The explosion of feeling that ran through her body was as intense as it had ever been. She must stop him before she made a fool of herself. With desperation Alice tore her mouth from his, curling her lips, her eyes flashing fire. 'What the devil do you think you're doing?' she demanded.

He smiled imperturbably. 'Trying to prove something. Keep still, will you.' And without more ado his lips claimed hers again, one hand coming up behind her head, and this time there was no escape.

Alice struggled fiercely but to no avail, and the longer the kiss lasted the more feeble became her efforts, and the sensations that rode through her body were a vivid reminder of the love she had once felt for him.

Desire flooded her loins, and as his kiss deepened and became more possessive and hungry she parted her lips and her hand slid automatically behind his neck.

This time it was Jared who called a halt. 'If you respond to Tony like that he's a lucky fellow,' he drawled.

'Don't be disgusting!' she spat.

'There's nothing wrong with sex with the right person so long as he *is* the right one?'

There was a question in his eyes, but Alice ignored it, hunching her shoulders and swinging away. She had once thought Jared was the right one.

She did not hear him leave the room, just the door closing quietly. She sank down on the bed. It had been six years, more or less to the day since he had first walked into her life.

'Mum, I'm home!' Alice skipped into the kitchen, slinging

her bag into the corner as usual, then coming to an abrupt halt when she saw her mother was not alone.

Who was this man? He was gorgeous. About twenty-eight with fantastic golden hair, thick and wavy, a tan that made her envious, and the bluest eyes she had ever seen.

He looked at her now and her mother made the introductions. 'This is Alice.' And to her daughter, 'I'd like you to meet Jared Duvall.' Gillian Alexander gave no explanation for his presence, but Alice thought she looked tense.

He held out his hand. 'I've been hearing all about you.'

It felt warm and strong, and Alice could not take her eyes off him. Who was he? Why was he here? And why was her heart racing like a mad thing?

Perhaps he was selling insurance? There were always salesmen knocking on the door. Or he might even be their new landlord. That was a strong possibility. They'd heard only the other day that old Mr Jones had sold most of his property and was retiring to Devon.

Of one thing she was sure, her mother wouldn't be interested in him, not as a man. He wouldn't make her mother's heart skip a beat. Disowned by her father when she became pregnant at the age of seventeen, deserted by the boy who had got her into that condition, Gillian Alexander had found life as a single parent very trying and very disillusioning. Her bitterness had grown over the years to such an extent that she showed no interest at all in the opposite sex.

Alice on the other hand, at sixteen, had a healthy awareness of boys, and this was the most devastating male animal she had ever come across. The fact that he was older than most boys of her acquaintance made him even more fascinating.

She smiled warmly at Jared Duvall. 'I hope it was good?'

'She made you sound like an angel.'

Alice glanced swiftly at her mother, wondering whether he was making fun of her.

But Gillian nodded. 'Alice is a great comfort to me. I couldn't ask for a better daughter.'

Jared Duvall's eyes lit up wickedly. 'You see, I wasn't lying.' His voice was extraordinarily deep and he had a way of looking at her that made her feel she was the most important person to him at this moment in time.

But there was exactly the same expression in his eyes when he glanced back at her mother. 'Gillian, how about that cup of tea?'

It must be a knack he had, of making everyone feel special, thought Alice. She found her curiosity growing and could not suppress an exciting awareness.

'I'll just go and wash and change, Mum, then I'll be back down.'

Alice decided on the green dress she had made the week before. She liked it because it made her look older. Dressmaking was a skill her mother had handed on to her, and she now made most of her own clothes.

She brushed her blonde hair, which she had washed only that morning. It was cut in a short, elfin style that suited her face. She debated whether to wear make-up then decided against it. She had a clear, almost translucent skin and wide blue eyes, and did not really needed any artificial aids. Besides, Jared might think she was trying to impress him, and maybe she was, but she didn't want him to know that.

They were still in the kitchen, her mother pouring the tea and Jared perched on one of the stools at the breakfast bar, a plate of biscuits in front of him. Whoever he was, he seemed to be making himself very much at home. He patted the stool next to him for Alice to sit down. 'Your mother tells me you're at college, learning hairdressing. Do you enjoy it?'

Alice smiled and nodded and looked into the deep blue of his eyes. How clear they were! 'It's what I've always wanted to do,' she told him.

'And then what, a few years in a top hairdresser's before opening your own salon?'

She rolled her eyes. 'Oh, that I could! But there'll never be enough money for that.'

'That's a defeatist attitude, Alice,' he said sternly. 'Aim high, that should be your motto.'

Easier said than done. He didn't know the way her mother had struggled over the years. As soon as Alice started work she intended handing most of her money over to her mother for improvements in the house, and perhaps a few luxuries like a holiday. They had never been away, except for day trips to the seaside. It was the very least she could do.

'Thank you, Gillian,' he said, as her mother set his tea down in front of him. Taking a biscuit from the plate, he stood up. 'Here, sit next to your daughter.'

'No, it's all right,' protested the older woman stiffly.

But Jared was adamant. 'I insist.' He moved round to the other side of the breakfast bar and stood facing them 'You're very much alike.' His eyes went from one to the other.

Alice looked at her mother and saw only the lines of weariness, the grey hairs mingling with the blonde, her work-worn hands. With a young daughter prone to illness—Alice had caught everything that was going during her childhood—Gillian had been unable to hold down a proper nine-to-five job. She did a few hours' cleaning here and there, and took in dressmaking, and somehow managed to feed and clothe them and pay the rent, never once complaining. There was a lot of love in their house, if nothing else.

'I imagine you're very proud of your daughter, Gillian?'

Jared remarked. 'She's a pretty girl and will break a few hearts before long, as I'm sure you must have done. Probably still do? You're a beautiful woman. You make a charming pair.'

What a flatterer he was! thought Alice, her eyes shining, but her mother didn't look pleased. In fact she looked as though she couldn't wait for him to leave.

After they had drunk their tea and he had demolished the plate of biscuits he said, 'How would you two girls like to go out to dinner tonight?'

Alice's eyes shot wide. This definitely couldn't be their landlord!

'I don't think so,' said Gillian, much to Alice's dismay.

'Nonsense,' he said. 'I've heard there's a super little restaurant just opened in town where the food is out of this world. I insist you come with me—I hate eating alone.'

'Oh, Mum,' Alice cried, 'we never go anywhere. Please say yes!'

But her mother was adamant. Perhaps, thought Alice, clutching at straws, it was because this man was dressed in an expensive mohair suit and Italian leather shoes, whereas her mother's dresses had sat in her wardrobe for years. She spent all her money on her daughter and the house.

'Some other time, maybe?' said Jared, looking genuinely disappointed. 'And now I must go. Thank you for your hospitality. It's been a pleasure meeting you, both of you.'

He kissed Gillian's brow, and the back of Alice's hand. She felt a bit like giggling. She had only ever seen that done in films.

When he had gone she looked at her mother. 'Wow! Where did he come from?'

'He's a friend of—of someone I once knew,' shrugged Gillian. 'He was in the area and came to look us up, that's all. I doubt we'll be seeing him again.'

'He's so dreamy,' said Alice. 'I do hope it's not the last we've seen of him. Who's this person who told him about us?'

'I don't want to discuss it,' insisted her mother firmly. 'And I don't want you getting any silly ideas about him. He's raked up some memories that I'd rather forget.'

Alice wisely held her tongue, but she thought she could guess what her mother meant. It was something to do with her teenage years, with the boy who had got her pregnant. Which meant there really was no chance that Jared Duvall would call again. Her mother must have made it very clear that she resented his calling on them. That was why she had looked so uptight when Alice got home. Only politeness had dictated that she entertain him

# CHAPTER TWO

ALICE was surprised, considering her mother's attitude, when Jared showed up at the house again a few days later. Surprised and pleased. In fact he came several times with gifts of flowers for her mother and chocolates for herself. She fantasised over him and because of her mother's continued coldness towards him decided it must be herself he came to see. The fact that he never singled her out for special treatment, and the fact that he and her mother shut themselves away in the front room and had long conversations, made no difference.

She got to the stage when she would rush home from college just to see him, and none of her friends would believe how handsome he was. They made excuses to call so that they could take a look at him themselves.

Her mother would never tell Alice what they had been talking about, and she always looked upset when he had gone. It was the first time she had not been completely open with her daughter. They had previously enjoyed an excellent relationship, able to speak frankly and intimately on any subject under the sun. On this subject only did her mother clam up, and Alice found it very hurtful.

On one occasion Jared brought his camera and took photographs of them both, and Alice insisted on having one with him, and she took one of Jared and her mother— even though her mother objected. When the films were developed Alice asked whether she might keep the one of her and him. She cut it up and put the pictures in her locket, and drooled over him whenever she was alone.

And then one weekend when Jared called her mother was out, so Alice made the tea and sat chatting to him. It was the first time they had been completely alone. Her heart skittered along at an alarming rate and she felt sure she was in love.

'So, Alice, tell me how you're doing with your hairdressing. Are you still enjoying it?'

'Very much,' she smiled, gazing rapturously into his eyes without even realising it.

'Are you experienced enough to have a go at this?' He touched a hand to his thick golden waves.

'Oh no, I couldn't. I wouldn't dare. What if I made a mess of it?' But the thought of standing so close, of actually touching him and having a legitimate excuse for doing so, was enough to bring swift colour to her cheeks and an added urgency to her heartbeat.

Jared looked amused. 'Have you not got that far?'

'Yes,' she admitted. 'I cut my mother's hair, and some of my friends', but I've never done a stranger's.'

'Is that how you see me?' The deep tones of his voice sounded infinitely sexy, or was she imagining it?

'Well no, not really, but I'd rather not.'

Jared did not press the matter, talking to her instead about her childhood. 'It's a pity you never had the pleasure of grandparents. Mine used to spoil me rotten, and I loved it.'

Alice jutted her chin. 'From what my mother's told me I've missed nothing. My grandparents had already split up when I was born, and I believe my grandmother died not long afterwards. But my grandfather wouldn't have loved me, even if he hadn't chucked my mother out—I'm quite sure of that. I hate him!' she finished angrily.

'Alice!' he rebuked gently. 'You don't know him. How can you say that?'

'I've heard enough about him. How could he possibly

have turned my mother out, can you tell me that? I can understand him being angry, and disappointed, but after all, she was his own flesh and blood. Couldn't he have used a little understanding?'

'Things were different in those days,' he said. 'Attitudes weren't so liberal. No one bats an eyelid at one-parent families today, but to have a baby out of wedlock when your mother was young was considered a sin.'

'I still think he was too hard on her, and I'm glad I've never met him,' she returned bitterly.

'Have you ever wondered who your father is?' Jared asked.

'Constantly,' she admitted, 'but that's one thing my mother refuses to tell me.' She paused, eyes narrowed, wondering if he could tell her. On the other hand, would she want to know? It had been a one-sided affair by all accounts. Her mother had loved the boy, but after he had bedded her he had lost interest. She hadn't even let him know that she was pregnant and had been adamant that his name should not be put on Alice's birth certificate.

'Poor Alice!'

'Poor Mother,' she corrected. 'She's the one who's suffered.'

'I know,' he said quietly. 'She's a remarkable woman. How would you like to go to the cinema?' he added.

Alice's lovely blue eyes widened. 'Are you serious?'

He nodded. 'I've never been more serious in my life.'

She had not needed asking twice, but if anyone had asked her what the film was about she would have been unable to tell them. She was so conscious of Jared at her side that everything else faded into oblivion.

He bought her popcorn and chocolates and lent her his handkerchief to wipe her fingers, and even wiped a smudge from the side of her mouth. But he didn't hold her hand as she would have liked. He smiled a lot, and he watched her, and his eyes were kind and unfathomable, and she felt good and wished he was in love with her too.

Afterwards they went to a café and had hamburgers and chips, and some of her friends were there and she saw them looking at her with envious eyes. When Jared took her home her mother was back, so she went straight up to her room and relived the past few hours over again.

For the whole of the next week Alice found it difficult to concentrate. Her body was a mass of sensation, her thoughts constantly on Jared. She ached with her love for him.

When, on the following Saturday, he turned up once more during her mother's absence Alice felt as though she were floating on Cloud Nine. They sat and talked, and he took her for a drive in his open-topped convertible, and the wind blew her hair and she laughed a lot. Then it rained and they struggled to pull over the hood.

All in all it was a very exciting day, one of the happiest she had ever spent, and when they returned home and her mother was still out, Alice turned to Jared with all her love for him shining in her eyes. 'Please kiss me, Jared,' she begged.

There was an instant of shock on his face, then he smiled gently and pressed a kiss to her brow.

'Not like that,' she cried, 'like this,' and she cradled his head in her hands and pressed her lips to his.

For a few seconds he did not move, then suddenly he groaned and his arms went around her and he kissed her, a deep, drugging, hungry kiss that was more mind-shattering than anything she had imagined in her wildest dreams.

She responded with complete abandonment, straining herself against him, her pounding heart echoed by his. How she had longed for this moment. What ecstasy! What undreamed-of excitement!

It was like the tearing away of her soul when he suddenly

thrust her from him. 'This is insanity!' he exclaimed harshly, his face pale beneath his tan. 'Alice, you don't know what you're asking of me.'

'I do,' she cried. 'I do!' Her face was ravaged by the pain of his rejection. 'I love you, Jared, I love you.'

He closed his eyes and took a deep breath and she saw that he was trembling.

'Can't you tell?' she went on. 'Haven't you guessed? Please, Jared, please say you love me too. You couldn't have kissed me like that and not meant it.'

She tried to touch him again, but he backed away from her, shaking his head, and there was no expression at all on his face. 'You don't know what you're saying, Alice.'

'Oh God, I do! I've dreamt about you, I've fantasised about you. I've wanted you ever since the first day I saw you. I was puzzled why you kept coming when it was clear my mother didn't welcome you, but now I know. You were waiting for an opportunity to get me on my own, weren't you? Please don't say it's not true, I couldn't stand it!'

'Alice,' Jared said gently, 'you're young and it's easy to imagine yourself in love, but——'

'I'm not imagining it!' she cried passionately. 'I do love you. Please, Jared, please don't do this to me!' The backs of her eyes ached with unshed tears.

Suddenly he was angry. His eyes flashed now and his mouth firmed. 'You're being stupid, Alice. You're still a child. You have a lot of growing up to do. You'll be in and out of love dozens of times before you're ready to commit yourself to a steady relationship. What you feel for me is nothing more than infatuation.'

'No, it's not,' she cried. 'I do love you, and I shall never love anyone else but you.' She placed her hand over her heart in a dramatic gesture, every ounce of feeling in those few words.

'Alice, for goodness' sake stop this foolish nonsense! Has your mother any idea how you feel?'

She shook her head miserably, some of the ebullience going out of her when she realised that he was serious.

'Then I think you should tell her; maybe she'll be able to talk some sense into you.' His tone was crisp and sharp and hurt her dreadfully.

'Is it my mother you love?' she demanded.

'Heavens, no! But she's a fine woman and I hope one day she finds the happiness she deserves. I'm going now, Alice, and I suggest you put this foolish episode right out of your mind.'

He walked out of the house then, and it was the last either of them saw of him. A letter arrived for her mother a few days later saying that he wouldn't be visiting them again, but thanking her for her hospitality and wishing them both every happiness and success in the future.

Alice shed buckets of tears and her mother guessed how she felt about him. 'I'm glad he's gone, Alice,' she said gently. 'He didn't make me very happy either.'

'I wish you'd tell me why.'

But her mother merely smiled and shook her head. 'He's best forgotten.'

'I hate him!' said Alice viciously.

Her mother wisely said nothing.

And now here he was again, and at long last Alice had found out why her mother had been upset by his visit. If only she had known, if only her mother had confided, she would never have let herself get involved.

For months after Jared's departure she had alternated between loving and hating him. A thousand times over she had relived every second they spent together, imagining his kisses, imagining whispered words of love, then going into fits of depression when she realised that he had never once given her any reason to believe he was in love with her. He had been kind to her because he felt sorry for her, for what she had missed out on, and she had mistaken his kindness for love.

She had had plenty of boyfriends since, but none had matched up to Jared. She had not loved any of them, their kisses had left her unmoved.

Realising she ought to be showering and changing instead of sitting here dreaming, Alice got up and opened her suitcase, quickly hanging her clothes in the wardrobe, then taking a few moments to admire the fantastic view.

Mainly it was mountainside, but if she hung her head out of the window she could glimpse the impossibly blue sea, and the sailing boats dotted here and there like exotic butterflies. She could not wait to swim and explore and find out more about this wonderful place.

Her bedroom was spacious and airy, and everything was painted white, and in the contrast the bathroom was a cool aquamarine. There was a bath as well as a shower and fluffy blue towels and a tiled floor, and a whole shelf full of cosmetics. For her? Or had her grandfather used to have frequent house-guests? She realised how little she knew about him.

The water was sheer heaven. She had felt hot and sticky, and now she pampered herself with expensive soap and matching talc, then dressed in a cool white cotton sundress that she had bought with the money the solicitor sent. And why not? she had asked herself when she went on her shopping spree. Wasn't that what the money was for? None of her wardrobe had been suitable for a holiday in the Caribbean.

Her hair was a lot longer now than when she first met Jared. It was heavy and shoulder-length, with a sheen of good health. It was her proudest asset. She brushed it carefully and decided she looked pretty good. She was ready to face Jared Duvall.

Tony was already downstairs. Alice found them sitting out on the terrace, which was in the shade at this time of day. It was still hot, though. The garden was a riot of colour and Alice thought she could see a pool through the trees. What bliss! For the first time she felt real regret that her mother had not healed the rift. What super holidays they could have spent here.

Jared and Tony were not speaking, which did not surprise her, They each sat wrapped in their own thoughts, but looked across immediately she emerged from the house.

Tony smiled, both relieved and pleased, but there was no emotion at all on Jared's face, not that she had expected any. He was as reluctant to entertain her as she to see him. He was the only flaw in this otherwise perfect place.

'Perhaps you'd like to be mother?' said Jared. There were biscuits on a plate, and it reminded her of the first time he had come to their house.

Her lips were compressed as she poured the tea. Why were memories so painful? Because he had hurt her, she told herself firmly. He had not cared about her own feelings. He was a cold-hearted brute. He had told her she was a child when she wasn't; he had said she didn't know her own mind. A child indeed!

Her eyes spat fire as she pushed his cup across the table. Six years hadn't lessened anything.

His lips quirked, as though he knew exactly what thoughts were running through her mind, and Alice turned deliberately to Tony. 'I'm glad you came,' she said.

He touched her hand across the table. 'I'm glad, too. This is really something!'

Jared's eyes glittered a metallic blue, but Alice ignored him.

'You should see the view from my bedroom, it's out of this world.'

'I'd love to,' said Tony. 'Mine looks over a courtyard.'

Alice slanted a glance at Jared. He wasn't looking at her, but there was a smug smile on his face and she could have kicked him. 'I'll show you afterwards,' she said. The smile disappeared.

They sipped their tea and nibbled biscuits, then Alice asked, 'Who's looking after the house?'

'A Mrs Bell,' answered Jared immediately. 'She came here when Mary died.'

Alice frowned. 'Who's Mary?'

'Dan's wife. He married again—but of course you wouldn't know that.' He looked at her speculatively for a second or two. 'She was a wonderful woman. You would have liked her. She could never do too much for anyone. She died last year, and Dan was broken-hearted. He was never the same after that. I've missed her too.'

There was so much she did not know, Alice realised. So much her mother hadn't known either. For a moment she felt sad, then she jutted her chin. She was not going to let Jared make her feel regret. Her grandfather had been at fault. He hadn't wanted them, and she was glad she had never met him.

'Is that a swimming pool over there?' she asked.

Jared nodded.

'In that case I think I'll go for a swim. Tony?'

'Most definitely,' he said, springing to his feet.

She gave him a brilliant smile and tucked her arm into his as they returned to the house to change. She did not look again at Jared, but could feel his eyes boring into her back. She wondered whether he would join them.

'I don't like that guy,' said Tony, the minute they were indoors.

'Nor me,' Alice confirmed sharply.

'What's he doing here anyway? He acts as though he owns the place.'

'Don't I know it!' Her eyes flashed hostilely. 'I can't

wait to go and see that solicitor and find out exactly what's going on.'

'Why didn't you tell me the truth about your mother and your grandfather?' Tony frowned. 'I had no idea you were——'

'A bastard?' suggested Alice brutally.

He flinched. 'Not that I care, you understand. Hell, it makes no difference these days.'

'But it did then,' she flamed. 'And I didn't tell you because it's no business of—anyone's, except mine.' She had told Tony nothing except that her mother and grandfather were not on speaking terms.

'But Alice, I want it to be my business. I love you. I——'

Alice cut him short. 'I'll see you in the pool. Don't be long.' And she raced along the corridor to her own room, closing the door and leaning back against it.

Tony's love was the last thing she wanted. Why did he have to complicate matters now? She had guessed he was getting serious, but nothing like this. How was she going to tell him? Perhaps she ought not to have let him come at all? It must have given him the wrong idea.

With less eagerness now, she pulled on her bikini which was also new, a brilliant jade-green and not very much of it. She grabbed a towel from the bathroom and ran down the stairs. Jared was still sitting on the terrace, and Alice did not know what made her do it, but she stopped and looked at him.

His appraisal was long and timeless, causing her body heat to rise and her heart to race. He began with her feet, working his way upwards slow inch by slow inch. At the top of her legs he paused, and the sensations in her loins were mind-blowing. Then on up again, over her stomach and her hips, pausing once more to feed on the swell of her breasts. It was torture and Alice knew she ought to run, but it was as though her legs were filled with lead and all she could do was stand and suffer his inspection.

How she wished she had pulled on a robe. This was awful! It was awakening all those feelings of six years ago, that dreadful time when she had sworn she loved Jared. Now she knew that he had been right and it had never been anything more than intense body chemistry. But it was still there, God help her. He still had that power to melt her bones.

His gaze was on her mouth now, which hung open and was dry, oh, so dry. She swallowed and licked her lips and with a strangled cry broke the spell. His mocking laugh followed her as she raced for the pool.

It was fantastic, looking as though it was a natural hollow in the mountainside, but she guessed it was man-made, hewn out of the rock to form this perfect place. The water was blessedly cold and took her breath away as she dived in. She forced herself to do several lengths before stopping and encountering Tony's puzzled brown eyes.

'What was all that about?' he wanted to know. 'Why the sudden spurt of energy?'

'It's him!' she cried. 'He makes me so angry. I just had to get him out of my system.' How pale Tony was compared to Jared, less muscular too. Jared's body was taut and toned and she would have loved to see him skimming through the water.

'And you've rid yourself of him?'

She nodded.

'So what happened? He stopped you on your way here? I wondered where you'd got to.'

'It was nothing really,' she shrugged. She could hardly tell him that all Jared had done was look at her. 'He just gets my back up. Oh, why did he have to be here? Why couldn't we have gone to see Mr Lewis this afternoon and got it over with? Then at least I'd know where I stand.' She hauled herself up and sat on the edge of the pool beside him.

The sun was warm on her back and it was so beautiful, with the palms and the brilliant shrubs, and the glittering water and the blue sky above, that she could have screamed because it was spoiled by Jared Duvall's presence.

'How well do you know Jared?' Tony rested his chin on her shoulder and nuzzled his nose into her cheek.

Alice wanted to move away, but she schooled herself to sit still. She did not want to hurt his feelings at this stage; she needed him. 'Not very well. I knew him for about three weeks, that was all.' A lifetime! She had met him, fallen in love with him, and had her love destroyed. The beginning and end, all within a matter of twenty-one days. But the memories had remained.

'How did you meet him?' His soft brown eyes were watching her closely.

She shrugged. 'He came to see my mother. I really had very little to do with him.' Twice he had taken her out, but how heavily she had fallen. Fancy her reading so much into it! He must have been laughing behind her back.

What sort of a report had he turned in to her grandfather? she wondered. 'Your sixteen-year-old granddaughter made a play for me, would you believe?' Had he said that? And had her grandfather believed she was no better than her mother, that she——Alice pulled herself up short. This was no way to go on.

'So why do you hate him so much?' Tony was like a terrier worrying a bone.

'Because he's here,' she snapped, finally moving away from him and sliding back down into the water. 'In this house. Come on, let's have a race.'

It was another half-hour before they finally made their way back indoors. The terrace was empty, the cups and saucers cleared away, and Alice took another shower and pulled the white dress back on. Presumably Mrs Bell would be cooking dinner, and how she was looking forward to it. She was ravenous. The only thing she wasn't looking forward to was seeing Jared again. But perhaps he had gone out? There had been no sign of him since they came out of the pool.

But it was wishful thinking on her part. When she went down the stairs he was at the bottom waiting for her. Gone were the shorts and casual shirt, replaced by cream slacks with a razor-sharp crease, and a beige silk shirt that emphasised the muscled hardness of his chest.

He led her into a room where the table was set for dinner, but the main feature was the far wall which was made entirely of glass, and the view was spectacular. It was as though they were perched on top of the world.

Alice went straight across to it and looked out. There was a sheer drop from the house down the mountainside, a riot of colour and texture with crooked palms and flowering trees, and birds swooping and calling, and butterflies hovering. And far, far below lay the rest of the island.

She had noticed when their plane came in to land what an intricate shape it was, and she could see now that they were in a huge sickle-shaped bay with all sorts of other little coves and islets on either side of them. What she had seen from her bedroom window was nothing compared to this, only one tiny fraction. Here was the whole fantastic panorama.

'Oh, Jared, it's breathtaking! I've never seen anything like it.' She turned shining blue eyes up to his face, forgetting for a moment the way she felt about him.

He smiled indulgently. 'You'd be hard pushed to find anything more spectacular.'

'I wish my mother had seen it,' she said quietly.

'So did your grandfather.'

Alice opened her mouth to protest, but he forestalled

her. 'Let's not go into that now.'

He was right, it was a pity to spoil these few moments. 'Where's Tony?' she asked. 'Has he seen this?'

Jared's mouth tightened. 'I have no idea where he is, and the less I see of that boy the better.'

Alice stiffened. 'What have you got against him?'

'He's come with you, isn't that enough?'

'You expected me to travel all this way alone?'

'Why not? You're a child no longer. You've grown, if I may say so, into a very beautiful and very confident young woman.' His eyes flickered briefly and appraisingly over her and she felt an immediate surge of awareness, gone instantly when he added, 'Whose idea was it, his or yours?'

She eyed him coldly. 'I don't see that it's anything to do with you, but actually it was Tony's, and I'm grateful, I should have hated it here alone.'

His brows rose. 'You've changed your mind about me? If I remember rightly the last time we met you declared undying love.'

'I was foolish,' she shrugged, 'as you rightly pointed out.' She had told herself that repeatedly, had actually believed it, until she met him again. Now it was all too clear that he could still affect her like no one else.

But it certainly wasn't love that she felt now, she was sure of that. He excited her, that was all. He seemed to be making her business his business, and she didn't like that, not one little bit.

'And it's Tony you're in love with at the moment?' His eyes watched her closely. 'How many more have there been?'

Alice tossed her head angrily. 'Too many to mention,' she lied. 'Stop quizzing me—my private life's none of your business!'

'Your grandfather would have wanted me to look after you.'

'Maybe so, but I don't. I've got Tony and I'm perfectly all right, thank you very much. If you've taken a day off from work just to welcome me then you needn't have bothered.'

'It was the least I could do,' he said, but the mocking tone of his voice infuriated her. Tony coming into the room was a welcome relief.

'Do come and look at the view,' said Alice, smiling widely and taking his arm, trying hard not to compare his faded jeans and T-shirt with Jared's ultra-smart clothes. 'It's fantastic!'

She clung to him religiously and ignored Jared, pointing out this and that, and pretending an affection she was far from feeling. She turned only when Jared suggested they take their seats at the table.

For the first time she took a good look at the room. The floor was polished wood with a Persian carpet in the centre, the furniture antique, probably imported at great expense from England. She had not realised her grandfather was so wealthy. Had he always been rich? She could not recall her mother saying anything about it. So how had he made his money? No doubt she would find out more about him tomorrow.

Jared sat her on his right, Tony on his left, himself at the head of the oval table. He really was taking over, wasn't he?

Mrs Bell turned out to be a dark-skinned middle-aged treasure, beaming all over her face, clearly delighted to have guests.

Alice had her first experience of turtle soup, but she did not like it very much; she guessed it was an acquired taste. It was followed by meatballs of some sort cooked in a rich, spicy sauce, accompanied by potatoes and peas. And then a refreshingly different pineapple tart which she found absolutely delicious. She drank only one glass of wine and refused a liqueur with her coffee.

All in all the meal was excellent, the company rather less so. Jared made no secret of the fact that he resented Tony's presence, and it was difficult to sustain a conversation when there was so much animosity. Alice was relieved when they finished and Jared disappeared. She and Tony pulled their chairs up to the window and exclaimed anew over the dramatic beauty of the scene below.

'I shan't want to go back home,' she said.

Tony agreed. 'You might not need to. If the old man's left you all this you can live here for the rest of your life.'

'I suppose I could,' she admitted, 'but somehow I don't think I will. I'd like to spend holidays here, though.'

'I could live here,' he said enthusiastically. 'I could really get used to this kind of life—swimming, snorkelling, windsurfing—I bet the sea's fantastic! Horse-riding, sailing. You'll make a mistake, Alice, if you give up all this. It's the opportunity of a lifetime. Promise me you'll think about it very carefully.'

She frowned. 'Why are you so adamant?'

'Alice, I love you.' His tone was indignant. 'Didn't you hear me earlier? And naturally I want the best for you.'

It was a nice thought, and a pity that she could not return his love. 'Tony,' she said hesitantly, knowing it was best to tell him now, 'I know I welcomed you coming with me, but—well, I'm not in love with you. I'm sorry, I didn't realise how you felt. You must think me pretty stupid. I thought we were just friends.'

'Say no more.' Tony touched her arm, his hand remaining there as he spoke. 'I do know how you feel, I assure you. I also know how I feel——' He pulled a wry face. 'I never intended telling you, not yet, not until you showed some signs of loving me in return, but I can't keep it to myself any longer. I have a chance, don't I? You wouldn't have asked me to come with you if you didn't feel something.'

'If I remember rightly,' said Alice with a slight frown, 'it was you who suggested coming.' Admittedly she had jumped at the offer but it certainly hadn't been her idea.

'Maybe I did,' he agreed easily, 'but only because I knew you were worried about travelling so far alone.'

'I was in a state,' admitted Alice. 'It was difficult coping after my mother died, and sometimes I didn't know what I was doing.'

But despite his kindness she still didn't love him, and she never would. Though perhaps right now wasn't the best moment to pursue it. Tony would realise in his own good time that her feelings were not the same as his.

'I'll always be at your side to help,' he said, gently kissing her cheek.

Alice did not speak, or move, and gradually silence settled between them. It had been a long, tiring and eventful day, and after a further half-hour she announced that she was going to bed.

'I think I might follow suit,' he said, standing also and catching hold of her hand. 'We should sleep like logs.'

They left the room and met Jared in the long hall. He glanced pointedly at their clasped hands. 'Where are you two going?' he asked.

'To bed,' they said in unison.

Thick brows rose and Alice knew exactly what he was thinking, but she had no intention of correcting his impression. 'Goodnight, Jared. What time do we need to leave tomorrow? Early?' She hoped so.

'We? Who is we?' A hard frown carved his brow.

'Me and Tony, of course.'

'Oh, no, Alice,' he said at once. 'This is private family business. You go alone.'

'Tony can wait outside,' she protested. 'Surely you

don't expect me to find my own way there?'

'Of course not, I'll take you myself.'

'While Tony waits here?'

He nodded grimly.

'That's not fair! If he comes he can have a look around the shops while he's waiting.'

'There are no shops,' returned Jared levelly. 'Mr Lewis operates from home. So you see how awkward it would be if you turned up with Tony? I'm sure he'll find something to amuse him here.'

He looked at the boy and Tony shrugged, his hands now shoved into his jeans pockets. 'I expect so,' he agreed.

'Good, I knew you'd see sense. Breakfast then at eight sharp, Alice. Would you like me to give you a call?'

'Would I hell!' she said beneath her breath. But she smiled faintly. 'No, thank you, I'll be ready.'

'Goodnight then, you two. Pleasant dreams.'

Jared watched them until they reached the top of the stairs. Tony headed off into his room after giving Alice a chaste peck on the cheek, and she walked out of Jared's sight down the corridor.

Alice felt sorely angry, but she was also desperately tired, and as soon as her head touched the pillow she was asleep.

# CHAPTER THREE

WHEN she awoke the next morning Alice had difficulty in remembering where she was. She gazed about the sunny, light room and thought she must be dreaming. Then it all came back with startling clarity. This was her grandfather's house, and it was the most beautiful place she had ever been in. The whole island had a magical air about it. The only two notes of discord were Jared Duvall and Tony Chatwin.

Jared she hated on two counts, one because he had deceived them when he came to England, and the other for the way he had humiliated her when she declared her love.

But today she was seeing the solicitor. Today she was going to learn exactly what it was her grandfather had left her. She jumped out of bed and stood for a moment at the window, drinking in the fragrance of the air and observing the breathtaking beauty of her surroundings. She spotted a lizard on the vine growing outside her window and watched entranced until he darted away.

After taking a shower she dressed in a straight white linen skirt and a crocheted cotton top, both of which she had made herself. She teamed them with red sandals and a narrow red belt, and a white straw bag with red flowers embroidered on it which had been a present from one of her girlfriends the Christmas before.

There was no sound from Tony's room as she walked past, and she wondered whether he was up or still asleep. His declaration of love really did disturb her. She had had no idea he felt this way. How could she have been so blind? It was no wonder he had offered to accompany her. He had obviously seen it as a romantic holiday, an opportunity to declare his feelings and persuade her that she loved him too.

With a sigh she carried on down the stairs, and Jared was waiting for her in the dining-room. He wore grey slacks and a white shirt and looked fresh and devastating. Alice tried to quell the sudden racing of her pulses. It was madness.

'Good morning, Alice.' His deep blue eyes appraised her thoroughly before coming to rest on her face. 'You slept well, I hope?'

'Yes, thank you,' she said quietly, taking her seat at the table. 'Is Tony up yet?' It was laid for the three of them.

'No.' The word was clipped and told her clearly that he had no wish to discuss the other man.

'I hope he'll be all right.'

'I'm sure he'll manage.' His sarcasm was thinly veiled.

'How long am I likely to be away?' Alice asked.

He shrugged. 'A couple of hours, maybe more.'

'I wish I knew what it was all about.'

A secret smile curved his lips, but he said nothing, simply pouring her a glass of fresh orange juice. She nibbled a crusty roll which she had spread lavishly with butter and honey, and felt a strange stirring inside her.

The news she was to receive in the next hour could make a world of difference to her life. On the other hand, her grandfather might have left her nothing. She must not overlook the possibility. He might have planned this merely to torment her, to show her what she had missed out on.

This aspect had not occurred to her before, but it suddenly assumed paramount importance. It was all some huge joke. There was absolutely no reason for him to leave her anything; he had never shown the remotest interest in her. She had been foolish to come. Her mother would have sent the ticket and money back with the contempt they deserved.

'I'll give you a dollar for them.'

Alice lifted her eyes to find Jared watching her. 'I don't want to go and see Mr Lewis. I want to go home.'

His brows rose. 'A fine time to make a decision like that! Why did you come, if that's how you feel?'

'I've only just realised what's going on,' she snapped. 'My grandfather's laughing in his grave, isn't he? He hasn't left me anything, it's just his way of emphasising the rift. He wants to show me what life could have been like if my mother had married well instead of shaming him by becoming pregnant.' A shudder ran through her. 'I'm sorry, Jared, I can't go through with it.'

Jared's lips firmed. 'You're being foolish, Alice, you're letting your mind run away with you. There's no reason at all to think that. You're his granddaughter, no matter what else might have happened. You're of his blood. He never forgot it.'

Alice pushed her chair back from the table, shaking her head wildly. 'Don't lie to me, Jared. I'm not going. I'm not going to be humiliated and made a fool of!'

'Alice, for pity's sake!' He rose angrily and stood in front of her. 'You must go. You owe it to yourself, and Daniel. He relented at the end, I know he won't mind me telling you that; he's not trying to hurt you.'

'And how would you know?' she asked coldly. 'You agreed it was a family matter. What the hell is it to do with you?'

'I was very fond of Daniel,' he said. 'Despite what you think, he was a good man. You must carry this thing through.'

He was right, of course. But if it was a hoax Jared Duvall had better look out. Alice shrugged and turned away. 'When do we go?' she asked flatly.

Tony was coming downstairs as they left the house. He had on his familiar uniform of T-shirt and faded jeans and looked like the poor relation. Alice smiled at him. 'We're just going,' she told him. 'I'll try not to be long.'

He did not look very happy and she guessed he did not like the idea of her going off with Jared. He needn't worry, she wasn't too keen on it herself. But what choice had she?

Jared's car was an old open-topped sports car that rattled and bumped over the uneven road surfaces. She was again reminded of when they had met six years ago. On the two Saturdays he had taken her out she had sat by him like this and felt the magic of being attracted to him. She had read so much into those few hours. How naïve she had been!

They wound their way down the mountain, Alice enchanted by sudden glimpses of white coves and blue seas, and she realised how stupid it would have been to turn round and go home without exploring this wildly beautiful place.

The solicitor's house was on the other side of the island. As the crow flies it was no more than a couple of miles, but the journey actually took them half an hour through some of the most enchanting countryside Alice had ever seen. She was too spellbound to speak, and Jared smiled at her rapt expression.

He dropped her off outside quite a plain house on the outskirts of a small village. 'I'm sorry I can't wait,' he told her, 'but Jim Lewis will see that you get back to Blue Vista.' And with gravel spurting from beneath his wheels he carried on along the road.

Alice watched him for a moment, then turned as a man came out of the house. He was short and rotund, with silver spectacles and a shiny bald head. He held out his hand. 'Miss Alexander?'

His grip was firm and he led her inside. She sat down in his office and clutched her bag on her knees and waited.

'Daniel has been sorely missed,' he said, his eyes pale and sad behind his glasses. 'He was well liked.'

Alice compressed her lips and said nothing.

'It upset him that you and your mother never came out to see him.'

She lifted her chin. 'I would say that was his fault, not ours.'

He nodded, closing his eyes for a moment. 'It was a sorry state of affairs.'

'I really don't want to discuss him,' said Alice. 'I'm here because you sent for me, so let's get on with it.'

He leaned back in his chair and rested his hands on his ample stomach. 'I think you ought to know more about Dan before we can do that.'

Alice felt herself growing impatient. 'Like what?'

'Tell me what you know about him so far.'

She frowned. 'What has that got to do with it?' When he didn't answer, she went on, 'Actually very little. Only what my mother told me, and as she hasn't seen him since the day he threw her out, that's not very much. I do know what type of a man he was, though—hard, unfeeling, totally unjust, capable of bearing a grudge for a whole lifetime. I think that's enough, don't you? I feel quite convinced that had we met I would never have felt any love for him.'

Jim Lewis shook his head. 'You're describing the old Daniel. When he first came here he was a broken man. He'd done wrong and he knew it, but he hadn't the courage to put things right. In other words, he'd run away. But no one can remain unhappy in these islands for long.'

Alice could agree with that. She had already felt their spell.

'He came here with a fair sum of money and set up his own charter business, ferrying tourists around the islands, etcetera, etcetera. He did really well, bought Blue Vista, became quite a celebrity. But then his health failed and he put in a manager to run the business for him, and soon after that things began to go wrong. The new man turned out to be crooked, and before Dan knew it he was out of business.'

'He was bankrupt?'

'I'm afraid so,' admitted the solicitor.

'So what am I doing here? What has he left me? The house and no money to run it?' Alice knew she sounded ungrateful, but it was useless pretending compassion she did not feel.

He shook his head. 'Blue Vista was one of the first things to go. He had so many debts that——'

She cut him short. 'Are you saying it doesn't belong to my grandfather?' Her heart began to pound and she had a feeling she knew what his answer was going to be.

'I'm sorry, no,' he answered with surprise. 'I thought Jared must have told you. It belongs to him. He bought it from Daniel many years ago.'

Alice drummed her fingers angrily on her bag. She felt like screaming. Jared should have told her. No way would she have stayed at Blue Vista if she had known! She wanted no favours from him.

'So where did my grandfather live after he'd sold?' she demanded heatedly. Some poky little cottage, she supposed, while Jared lorded it up at the big house.

Jim Lewis looked surprised. 'He stayed on at Blue Vista, of course. Jared wouldn't have let him do otherwise. They were good friends.'

'Friends? How did they become friends?' It seemed an unlikely sort of relationship to her, considering the difference in their ages.

'It happened when Jared was in the Bahamian police force. Dan had some trouble with one of his ships being broken into in Nassau. Jared actually caught the men who did it and they've been friends ever since. More like father and son, actually.'

Father and son? The thought hurt. Jared had taken the place in Daniel's life that should have been her mother's. The more she heard about this man the more she disliked him. 'Is Jared still a policeman?' she asked.

'Heavens, no! He left after ten years. He now runs his own highly successful security business.'

'I see,' she said.

'You know about Mary?' he asked, abruptly changing the subject.

'My grandfather's second wife?'

Mr Lewis nodded.

'I didn't, until Jared mentioned her. It was quite a shock. I'm sure my mother never knew either.'

'She was Dan's housekeeper originally, but they fell in love and got married, and when Jared bought the house she carried on looking after it for him.'

'And my grandfather did all the odd jobs and tended the gardens, I suppose? Some purchase, wasn't it? Did they come in with the price?'

'Don't be angry,' said the solicitor gently. 'It was a perfect arrangement, and Luke loved Mary too. He was so distressed when she died. She was like a mother to him.'

Alice frowned. 'Luke?' Who on earth was he?

Jim Lewis shook his head in disbelief. 'Jared hasn't told you about him either?'

'He said the reason I was here was family business and nothing to do with him.'

'So it is, but I can't believe he hasn't told you about Luke. Luke is his son.'

Alice did not know whether she could take any more

shocks today. Jared had a son! Jared was married? A cold hand clutched at her heart, even though she knew it ought to make no difference. She had learned to hate him, the only feelings she had for him were physical—and they could be ignored. So why did she feel this bitter disappointment? Why had her throat closed up and speech become impossible?

'You didn't know?'

She shook her head.

'He's away at school at the moment, but he'll be home soon for the holidays. He's a very lovable boy.'

Alice doubted she'd still be here, but she did not voice her thoughts. 'How old is Luke?' she asked instead.

Jim Lewis smiled. 'He's almost six.' And it was clear he had soft spot for the boy.

Which meant Jared must have been married when he came to England? The hand clutched her heart even more tightly. It made everything so much worse. Why hadn't he said? Why had he encouraged her? Why had he let her throw herself at him?

No, that was wrong, he hadn't encouraged her. He had merely been kind and attentive and she had read more into it than there was. But it was still his fault, he should have seen what was happening and stopped it.

'Where's his wife now?' she asked. Lord, she hoped she didn't have to meet the woman.

'They're divorced,' admitted the solicitor quietly.

'And Jared has custody of the child?'

Mr Lewis nodded. 'That's right.'

Alice felt her anger growing. 'And yet he's sent him away to school at that tender age? My God, what sort of a man is he?'

'There are reasons,' said Jim Lewis softly.

But of course he'd say that. He was on Jared's side. Reasons like the lad interfered with his work. Reasons like having a six-year-old son around ruined his social life. Alice snorted. 'I don't think I want to discuss this any more. I think it's time you told me the real reason I'm here.' Though now she had discovered her grandfather had died penniless, she could not imagine what it was.

Gravely he handed her an envelope. Alice frowned and looked at him questioningly.

'Your grandfather instructed me to give you this. He wrote it the day your letter came about your mother. He was deeply upset. He'd always hoped that one day a reconciliation would take place, and when he knew it was too late his heart gave up. He died peacefully in his chair less than forty-eight hours later. Jared was talking to him one moment, the next he'd gone.'

Alice felt a twinge of pity, but stamped on it firmly. Her grandfather should have made the move earlier if he'd wanted forgiveness. Sixteen years he had waited to find out if they were all right. Her mother's bitterness had grown over those years until nothing could shift it.

She fingered the envelope and took the paper-knife Jim Lewis offered her, slitting it and withdrawing the single sheet of paper.

'Dear Alice,' she read, 'One of my deepest regrets in life is that you and I have never met. You are my grand-daughter and yet I don't know you. I admit it was all my fault, but I have tried to make amends. I did write to your mother.'

Had he? Alice paused a moment, frowning. It was the first she had heard of it. He must be lying. Her lips firmed.

'I've never been more content than in these islands, and my only sorrow is that you and your mother weren't here to enjoy them with me. It would have made my happiness complete.

'But Alice, my dear, it's not too late for you. I want

you to do something for me. I want you to make Blue Vista your home for the next three months.'

Alice gasped. Did he know what he was asking?

'I know Jared won't mind—he spoke about you highly after returning from England. And during your time here I'm sure you will learn to love the place as much as I do.'

Alice paused again and looked across at Jim Lewis. He was watching her closely. 'You've finished?'

'Not yet,' she said, swallowing hard. 'But it's preposterous. I really can't do this. I can't!'

'Read on,' he said, in his quiet soothing tone.

She looked down again at the paper and realised her hands were trembling.

'If you then decide to make this island your home you will benefit under the terms of my will. If you go back to England it will be your loss.

'My very best regards to you—Daniel Alexander'

'This is blackmail!' she cried, her eyes widening as she read the last paragraph again.

'Dan wanted you to enjoy what he has enjoyed,' said the solicitor. 'He loved it here very much. I was asked to do my best to make sure you conformed to his request.'

'And if I don't?'

'As he said, there'll be nothing for you. And Daniel will have swallowed his last ounce of pride for nothing.'

Alice shook her head, still bemused. 'But I thought he was penniless? What had he got left to leave?'

'There was some money,' he told her. 'Not much, admittedly. He left most of it in a trust for Luke and——'

'For Luke?' she butted in incredulously.

He nodded. 'That's right. You're forgetting they were the family he hadn't got.'

'He didn't want to know his natural family,' protested Alice. 'My God, the more I hear the more I realise my mother was right. He was a monster!'

The solicitor leaned forward on his desk, resting his chin on his fingertips and looking at her sadly. 'You would never say that if you'd known Daniel,' he assured her.

'I'm glad I didn't know him,' she said firmly.

'But you will think about what he's asked?'

'It's impossible!' she cried. 'I'd lose my job to start with, and they're not easy to get these days.'

'I think that's a very small price to pay.'

'Oh, you do, do you?' Alice's eyes flashed blue. 'You're nice and secure here, I can see that. But if I lose my job how am I going to pay the rent? And more to the point, how would I pay it for the three months that I'm here? I can't let the house go, I wouldn't find anywhere else like it. Besides, I've lived there all my life and I don't particularly want to move.'

'I'm sure something can be arranged,' he said smoothly.

'Oh, yes, like Jared paying for it. Conscience money because his family's benefited and I haven't. I can't do it, Mr Lewis, I'm sorry. This has been a whole waste of time. What stopped you posting my grandfather's letter?' she added. 'My answer would have been no different.'

He reached across the desk and touched her hand. 'Calm down, Alice—I may call you that? I realise this has been a bit of a shock, but once you've had time to think it over you'll realise exactly what you're being offered. A three-month holiday, to start off with. You won't have to find a penny, it's all been provided for. And after that—well, who knows?'

'Do *you* know?' she demanded.

He shook his head. 'Not entirely. The answer is locked away in my safe. My advice to you is to take a few days to think about it and then come and see me again.'

Alice sat silent, shaking her head, looking all about the room, as if seeking an answer to her problem. 'I have a friend with me,' she said abruptly.

Mr Lewis looked surprised. 'I'm afraid that unless she can pay her own way your grandfather's terms don't provide for anyone else.'

'It's a he.'

His eyes widened. 'Your boyfriend?' His eyes flickered down to her ringless wedding finger.

She shrugged. 'Not really.'

'Then you wouldn't be too upset if he went back?'

No, but Tony would. He would not like it, not one little bit. He loved it here already. 'I doubt if he'll be going alone,' she said quietly.

'We'll see,' he replied, rising to his feet, 'and now I'm afraid I have another client due. There's a taxi outside. It will take you straight back to Jared's house.'

Jared's house. The words grated on her nerves. It was her grandfather's house, and it should have been hers, as well as everything in it. Trust Jared to jump in the moment her grandfather was down! He had probably thought he was doing Daniel a favour by letting him stay on. How it must have hurt being a servant in the house that was once his own!

The journey back to Blue Vista was nothing like the outward one. Alice saw nothing, her mind totally taken up by Daniel Alexander's strange request. Could she do it? Would she? Was it wise? Would it be worth it? Oh, lord, what a predicament she was in!

All this way she had come, to be told that her inheritance depended on whether she stayed here for three months. And would it be worth it in the end? Who knew? No one, it seemed, except Daniel, and Daniel had taken his secret to the grave with him.

Arriving back at Blue Vista, she looked for Tony, wondering exactly how to tell him what had transpired. He would be as astonished as she. They had both been under the impression that this house and all her grandfather's money would be coming to her. What a let-down!

Mrs Bell told her that Tony had gone exploring. Alice could not blame him. He never had liked his own company. He must have been bored out of his mind.

She was hot and sticky as well as fuming, so she went for a swim, then, still too restless to sit and do nothing, she began to explore the house. It really was beautiful. She discovered a big comfortable lounge and one table was full of photographs in fancy frames.

There was Jared by himself, looking devilishly handsome, she had to admit. Jared with his son, she presumed—a mischievous-looking boy with a grin that nearly split his face in two. There were the pictures Jared had taken of her and her mother. Why were they here? And finally a photograph of an older man who she presumed was her grandfather.

She picked it up and studied it more closely, reluctantly admitting that he did not look the ogre her mother had made out. He looked a kind man, one who would love his children and grandchildren, play with them, amuse them, spend many hours with them. Who said the camera couldn't lie? He wasn't like that at all. Hadn't he proved it beyond any shadow of doubt? Alice felt her temper beginning to rise again, and she slammed the photo down and carried on with her tour of the house.

It was cleverly designed. It was built in a U-shape with the inner courtyard guarded by the mountain in which the house was set.

All the rooms at the front had that marvellous view of the bay; the side ones looked across the mountains, but if you leaned out of the windows you could still catch tantalising glimpses of the water. The rest overlooked the courtyard, which in itself was not unpleasant with a fountain and shrubs in tubs, and vines and statues and an ornately tiled floor.

The pool was at one side of the house where the main gardens were, and it looked as though it was a natural part of the landscape. How cleverly it had been fitted into the general theme!

Eventually Tony came back. Alice was sitting in the garden beneath the shade of a flamboyant tree. He looked disgruntled, and she was sorry she hadn't better news. For the last hour she had deliberately pushed all thoughts of her grandfather's request from her mind, too confused to know what decision to take. She was relying on Tony to help her make the right one.

He dropped down on to a canvas chair beside her, smiling now and putting his arm along the back of her seat. 'Well, darling, how did it go?'

She grimaced. 'Not exactly as I expected.'

'No?' His brows rose. 'So, what's the old guy left you?'

'I don't know,' Alice said quietly.

This time he frowned. 'What do you mean?'

'Well, there's a condition.'

'What sort of a condition?'

She took a breath and said quickly, 'I'm to stay here for three months before I get anything.' And even then she had to settle here permanently, but she wasn't going to tell him that because she knew he would want to stay with her. It would be no hardship to Tony; he loved the place already. As well as her! It had been a mistake letting him come in the first place, she realised that now.

'My God, the man was insane! He can't mean that? You must contest it. It's ridiculous! I've never heard anything like it in all my life. Alice,' he looked at her closely, 'you're not going to go along with it?'

'What else can I do?'

'As I said, contest it.'

'I don't think I can.'

Tony shook his head in disbelief. 'How can you say that?

Why is he making you wait three months? His money's yours, this house is yours, why can't you have it now? Hasn't he caused enough anguish in your life, that he has to continue even now he's dead?'

'It's not quite like that,' she explained. 'For a start, this house belongs to Jared. He bought it from my grandfather when he ran into financial difficulties.'

Tony stilled.

'I thought that would shock you,' Alice grimaced wryly. 'It did me. I hate having to accept favours from Jared.'

'I hardly think that's the point,' said Tony tersely. 'He bought this house from your grandfather, you say?'

She nodded.

'And it's my guess he took your grandfather for a ride and paid only a nominal amount for it.'

'Hold on,' said Alice. 'Why do you say that?'

'Because that's the type he is. Can't you see that? If he's fiddled you out of your rightful inheritance, I shall make it my duty to expose him. How about your grandfather's money—you are getting that, I presume?'

She pulled a wry face. 'What there's left of it, I imagine. But most of it has been put into trust for Jared's son.'

'His son?' Tony jumped to his feet and glared down at her. 'Alice, this is beyond a joke! You're not going to sit back and accept it?'

'I haven't decided yet what I'm going to do,' she said with quiet dignity. 'And I don't see why you're getting so worked up. It's my problem, not yours.'

'I care about you, Alice. Who the hell's going to look after your interests if not me? It's obvious that Jared set out to line his own pockets. Can't you see that?'

'I don't think that's true,' she said. But she realised she had been as near to thinking the same thing herself. To hear Tony say it, though, was something else. 'It would appear that Jared did my grandfather a favour by buying this house and then letting him stay on. They were very close, like father and son.'

Tony snorted. 'He made sure of that!'

Alice shook her head. 'I can't see why you're letting it bother you.'

'It bothers me,' he raged, 'because I've wasted my hard-earned money coming here. You're forgetting I didn't have a free ticket like you.'

Her eyes opened wide. 'Don't blame me, Tony; it was your idea, and you know it.' Goodness, what had got into him?

'I'm sorry, I didn't mean that.' He looked distraught by his own insensitivity. 'I wanted to come with you, I really did. It's just that I know how disappointed you must be. I feel for you, Alice—you, not myself.'

He dropped to his knees in front of her and took her hands into his own. 'Don't let them make a fool of you,' he said earnestly.

'I won't,' she said quietly, accepting his apology. She knew how easy it was to say the wrong thing when you were in a temper.

Jared returned home at lunch time, and to Alice's chagrin he did not ask how she had got on at the solicitor's. Though had he done so she would have told him to mind his own business. Perhaps he knew that?

But she could not keep silent about Blue Vista. 'Why didn't you tell me this house was yours?'

His mouth twisted cynically. 'Because you wouldn't have stayed here. Isn't that right?'

She nodded, her teeth clenched. 'Was my grandfather really so down that you had to buy it from him?'

A fleeting shadow crossed his face. 'He was.'

'Did you give him a fair price?'

'I doubt it,' interjected Tony, his eyes condemning as he glanced at the older man and then back to Alice. 'He'd probably always coveted it and made some ridiculous offer because he knew your grandfather wasn't in any position to say no.'

Alice was appalled by Tony's display of bad manners, but Jared was ten times more so. His face darkened angrily, his eyes glittered. 'When I want your opinion, Chatwin, I'll ask for it! This conversation has nothing at all to do with you, and I'd thank you to keep your nose out of it.'

'Hasn't it?' demanded Tony, his face now flushed an ugly red. 'I'm here to protect Alice, and the way I see things——'

'That's enough!' Jared's crisp tone silenced him. 'Alice doesn't need you. She doesn't need protection. No one's trying to take advantage of her.'

'No?' questioned Tony loudly. 'She came here expecting to inherit a fortune and what does she get? Nothing! No house, no money, not a thing. What I want to know is, where has it all gone?'

There was an icy calm about Jared that should have warned Tony, but instead he went on, 'It's my guess that it's you who fleeced him, but it's not going to stop there. I've told Alice to contest the will. She has a right to her grandfather's estate. I won't let her sit back and do nothing. I don't suppose you or your son even need the damn money, it's just greed, it's——'

'Tony, shut up!' Alice looked at him, agonised. What was wrong with him?

'I won't shut up,' he roared. 'This man's taking you for a ride, and——'

'Didn't you hear what Alice said?' Jared's voice in complete contrast was quite calm, but there was a steel edge to it and his controlled temper was more to be feared than Tony's blustering rage.

'Please, Tony, I think you've said enough.' She touched

his arm, but he angrily thrust her hand away.

'I'm not going to let you stay on for three months when it might not be worth it.'

'*You're* not going to let her stay on?' barked Jared. 'What the hell's it to do with you?'

'Everything,' defended Tony. 'I love Alice. I want to marry her.'

Alice felt her mouth drop open and Jared's thick brows shot up. 'Now that does surprise me,' he drawled. 'You'd marry her—even though there's no house, no money? Or are you still hoping there'll be something in the end?'

Tony's eyes flickered before he masked them and glared defiantly at the older man. 'I'm interested only in Alice's happiness.'

'Not in the state of her bank account?'

'I have a good job,' Tony defended. 'Why should I be?'

'Why indeed?' crisped Jared. 'But my instincts tell me you are.'

'I don't have to take this from you!' snarled Tony.

'And I don't have to give you a roof over your head. If I were you, Chatwin, I'd hold my tongue.'

Alice was still grappling with the shock of learning that Tony wanted to marry her and she glanced from one to the other hardly listening. Had Tony meant it? Was he that serious about her? Why hadn't he told her instead of blurting it out in front of Jared like this?

She wished now that she had been more insistent when she said she didn't love him. He obviously hadn't believed her, or at least he had thought it would only be a matter of time before she changed her mind. He must have gone on thinking that there was still a chance and he had taken this opportunity to try and force her hand.

But she could not accept that Jared was right and Tony was simply after her inheritance. He knew there was nothing left. Hadn't she told him that? He loved her. It was that simple, and here they were arguing like a couple of schoolboys.

'Stop it, you two. *Stop it!*' she shouted, suddenly galvanised into action.

They looked at her and Tony mumbled a few incoherent words, then left the room. Jared's eyes were cold. 'Congratulations.'

'On what?' A frown creased her normally smooth brow.

'Your forthcoming marriage.'

# CHAPTER FOUR

ALICE inhaled deeply and, deliberately turning her back on Jared, she stared out of the window.

'I must confess you don't look very happy about Tony's proposal.' He came up behind her, and she could feel the warmth of him and smell the maleness of him, and tiny frissons of awareness ran right down the centre of her.

'I wonder if he affects you as I do?' he asked, his voice low and close to her ear. 'If you want my opinion, I think you'd be making a big mistake.' He slid his arms around her waist and pulled her against him. 'And I think I should show you yet again what it's like to be kissed by a real man.'

The very thought of it set Alice's heart pounding, but still she struggled frantically. This was insanity! 'Get away from me, Jared—don't touch me!'

But his arms tightened. 'There's no point in fighting, Alice.' His mouth was against her ear, nibbling her lobe, kissing the soft area behind it, creating havoc with her senses.

She closed her eyes and let insanity take over for a few seconds. He did not have to prove to her that he was a better man than Tony. She knew it already.

'It was a strange sort of proposal. Are you going to accept?'

Was she going to marry Tony? No. She was about to deny it emphatically when the realisation came to her that Tony could be her defence, the buffer she needed against Jared.

She nodded.

'You're insane!' He spun her round in his arms and looked deep into her eyes for a brief space before claiming her lips with a savagery that turned hell loose inside Alice.

'Does he affect you like this? Do you respond to him as you do to me?' he demanded.

She fought desperately. She must not let Jared do this. She must not let him get through to her.

'Don't fight me, Alice,' he gritted against her mouth, 'You want this as much as I do.'

'No!' She shook her head desperately.

'Yes,' he insisted, and the pressure of his lips increased.

Alice's heart thudded and an impossible warmth heated her skin. Had he any idea at all of the chaos he was creating inside her? Her heartbeats were almost painful in their intensity. It was sheer madness. She must stop him.

She forced her hands between them and pushed with all her might, but it was useless.

'Jared!' she implored.

'Alice,' he mocked.

'Please let me go.'

'Why?' He tightened his arms about her waist so that their thighs welded and her loins felt on fire.

'I want you to.'

'And I want to hold you—like this, and kiss you—like this.' His mouth closed yet again on hers and this time his kisses were hungry and urgent and demanded a response, and Alice could not help herself. Her arms wound around him; her fingers clawed through his hair, holding his head close, drinking the throbbing maleness of him and knowing it was insane, yet unable to do anything about it. It was crazy responding to a man who meant nothing to her, and yet she hungered for him. The past six years had not diminished her desire. It was a crazy, mixed-up sexual need that ought never to have seen the light of day.

'Why didn't you tell me you were married when you

came to England?' The sound of her own voice startled her.

He did not stop kissing her, and his voice was muffled as he answered. 'It didn't seem necessary.'

'But it was why you rejected me?' she insisted. If he said yes she would admit here and now that she did not love Tony, that she loved him still. Because surely he loved her? Surely he wasn't kissing her like this for nothing?

'No, it wasn't,' he admitted. 'I never intended that you should fall in love with me, Alice.' He had lifted his head now and his voice was firm and clear.

Because he had been in love with his wife? Alice felt crushed. And they had had a son not long afterwards. And now they were divorced. So what had gone wrong? How dearly she would have loved to ask, but she had said enough. She should never have mentioned his marriage. It was clear now that he had never felt anything for her.

With a strangled cry she finally managed to break away. But already she had revealed her feelings, and there was an expression on his face she could not read, and desire in his eyes that sent still more excitement coursing through her limbs.

And in that moment she knew that it would be impossible to remain here for three months. They would end up being lovers, despite the fact that she had said she was marrying Tony, and when it was all over she would hate Jared more than ever. Whatever it was her grandfather wanted her to have, he could keep it. The price was too much to pay.

Lunch on the terrace was a silent affair. Tony sulked, Jared had a perpetual secret smile, and Alice was torn between compassion for Tony and an increased awareness of Jared. She was glad when he went back to work.

They sat on at the table and the silence continued. Tony toyed with his fork and Alice watched him. 'You *were* very rude,' she said at length.

He lifted heavy eyelids. 'I was speaking the truth.'

'You're an uninvited guest, don't forget.'

'That's easily remedied,' he sneered. 'I'll pack up and find a room somewhere else, and you can come with me.'

'Tony, no! What's the matter with you? What's happening? Why are you behaving like this?'

He groaned and held his head in his hands. 'Hell, I don't know.' Then he looked at her and his eyes were pained. 'Yes, I do. I'm jealous of Jared, if you must know. He has so much that I'm afraid you'll transfer your affections.'

'And was that why you said you wanted to marry me?'

He nodded. 'It was a stupid thing to say, I realise that now. I suppose you told him you didn't love me?'

'Actually, no,' she said.

Tony's eyes widened.

'Because I felt it would keep him off my back,' she admitted. 'Do you mind?'

'Mind? Hell, no.' He was actually smiling. 'You've done me a favour. You've stopped me looking a fool, and now I shan't give up hope. I do love you, Alice, really I do. Just tell me one thing. Do you love Jared?'

'*No!*' Alice's response was instantaneous and she surprised even herself by her vehemence. 'I could never love Jared. I hate him!'

'Then how come I saw you kissing him, Alice? And it was nothing like the pecks you give me.'

She felt the blood rush to her cheeks and she avoided looking at him. 'He forced me. I couldn't escape.'

'You looked to me as though you were enjoying it,' Tony said drily.

Oh lord, she had been. Even now a swift thrill rode through her at the mere thought of Jared's kisses. But she denied it blatantly. 'I couldn't move. He was too strong for me.'

'If you want my honest opinion,' he said, 'I think it's Jared who's the gold-digger. I think the reason he's trying to blacken me in your eyes is because he's after whatever your grandfather left. And if that means marrying you then he'll do just that.'

'Tony, no—how can you say that? Jared doesn't need more money; he's wealthy in his own right.'

'And how did he get it? Tricking your grandfather out of this house, for starters. He's probably been feeding off him for years.'

'For heaven's sake, Tony, there *is* no vast fortune,' Alice explained. 'We've come on a fool's errand, if the truth's known. All I'm likely to get out of it's a three-month everything-paid-for holiday and maybe a small sum of money.'

'I'm not so sure,' he said slowly. 'I can't see the old man bringing you all this way for nothing. I think there's more to it. And I think you're doing the right thing in staying. I've half a mind to pack up my job and stay with you. I've a bit of money saved and I could always do some work here. What do you say, Alice?'

Alice almost told him then that she had changed her mind, that she had decided to leave after all. But how could she, without admitting the truth about Jared?

'It seems a very final thing to do,' she said. 'You might get fed up after a while. I know it's very new and exciting at the moment, but it won't last.'

'You don't want me here, is that it?' he demanded, his tone aggressive.

'Tony, stop jumping to conclusions!' Alice strove for patience. 'Two days is no time at all to make up your mind.'

'I know I want to marry you,' he insisted.

She groaned inwardly. 'Let's not talk about that.'

'But we are good friends,' he insisted. 'We always have

been, haven't we? We've never argued, we've always got on well together. I think that's a very good foundation. I think that in time you'll realise it is love you feel for me.'

Would he never give up? Alice pushed back her chair. 'I don't want to discuss this any more.'

Immediately he was repentant. 'I'm sorry. It was never my intention to rush you. It was Jared who forced my hand.'

Her blue eyes widened. 'I don't see how.'

'I simply wanted to make it clear that it's you I'm interested in, not your inheritance.'

Alice shook her head. 'He's wrong about you, and you're wrong about him. Let me tell you the whole story, and then you'll see why.'

'I don't particularly want to hear it,' said Tony gruffly.

'I think you should,' she said.

He shrugged, and waited uninterestedly.

'Several years ago,' explained Alice, 'my grandfather fell ill. I think it must have been about the time he sent Jared over to England. He had his own highly successful charter business and he put in a manager to run it. That man did him out of every penny he possessed. My grandfather even had to sell this house to pay his debts.'

Tony eyed her sceptically. 'You mean to tell me your grandfather didn't see what was going on?'

'He was ill, don't forget. And he trusted the man.'

'He sounds like a fool to me,' jeered Tony.

Alice ignored him. 'Jared bought this house from my grandfather and let him and his wife go on living here for nothing. Jared apparently has his own security firm. He's not short. He didn't fleece Daniel, he helped him.'

'I still think he has designs on you,' said Tony.

Alice stood up in exasperation. 'You think what you want to think, Tony. I'm going for a walk in the garden—alone.'

'Alice, you can't blame me! He's made it clear ever since we arrived that I'm not welcome, and then I see him kissing you. What am I supposed to think?'

'Not that he has any designs on me,' she snapped. 'None at all.' And with that she flounced away.

She half expected Tony to follow, but there was no sign of him when she reached the pool and sat down. It was tranquil here, and she tried to push all unpleasant thoughts from her mind.

Somewhere she heard a frog croaking and saw several lizards fly-catching. They were fascinating. And a yellow-breasted bird came to look at her, and on the rooftop a dove cooed.

She closed her eyes and let her thoughts wander. Was Tony really serious about staying on? Could she manage another ninety days of continual hostility between him and Jared? Would Jared let him live here or would he need to find rooms?

And she still hadn't told Tony that to fulfil the terms of Daniel Alexander's will she would have to settle here for the rest of her life. Not that Tony was interested in the money, she didn't believe that for one moment, but he did want to marry her. Could he, though, seriously face the thought of living here for ever? It was all very well fantasising about it after two days, but a whole lifetime was a different story. He might not be so keen.

She also wondered what it would be like to stay here without Tony. Say, for instance, she had come alone and found Jared? At one time she would have been in seventh heaven. She had loved him unreservedly, with the blind, adulatory love of a teenager. But his rejection had altered all that, and although her feelings had not changed she could never forgive him. He should have told her from the start that he was married. He should never have let her fall in love.

It was hot now, too hot to stay out of doors. She went up to her room and lay down on the bed, and the next thing she knew Jared was shaking her shoulder.

Instantly she was wide awake and wondering at his nerve in coming into her room.

'Dinner will be ready in half an hour,' he told her.

'Thanks,' she said, and when he remained looking down at her, she added, 'You can go now, I won't fall asleep again.' She could not imagine how she had slept so long in the first place.

'What have you been saying to Chatwin?' he wanted to know.

Alice frowned and sat up. 'Why?'

'He doesn't look much like a man who's just got engaged.'

She shrugged. 'We talked, that was all. I explained a few things to him.'

'Such as?'

'That you're not after my grandfather's money.'

'But he is?'

'No!' she answered quickly. 'Heavens, what is it with you two?' She swung her legs over the edge of the bed, tugging down her skirt which had risen half-way up her thighs. A fact Jared had not missed.

'Shall I tell you what's wrong with him?' he demanded, and without waiting for her to reply, 'Tony's afraid I might steal you from him, you and your inheritance.'

It was so near to the truth that Alice could not deny it. 'And what are you afraid of?' she asked airily.

'Not a lot,' he smiled, pausing a moment and looking at her with that half grave, half mocking way he had. Alice's insides began to stir and she gripped the edge of the bed. 'But I think Tony needs careful watching. He's serious about your grandfather's money.'

'Nonsense!' Alice swivelled her eyes heavenwards. 'I've

explained to him that there's hardly anything left. So how can you say that?'

'He doesn't believe you. He sees only this fine house, the life-style that was your grandfather's until misfortune befell him. He can't accept that it was all a thing of the past.'

'He believes you swindled him out of it!' she shot.

'So I gathered,' said Jared drily.

'I told him it wasn't true. I explained the position more clearly to him.'

'So what's he going to do, and, more to the point, what are *you* going to do? Are you staying here for the stipulated three months?'

'I've not yet made up my mind,' she answered firmly, then wondered why she had said that.

'I hadn't realised the decision would be so difficult.'

'Let's say that if you weren't here there would be no decision to make.'

His eyes narrowed. 'Maybe I should apologise?'

'Maybe you should have told me who you were when you came to England.'

'Your mother wouldn't let me,' he said quietly.

Alice clamped her lips.

'So,' he went on, 'let's say you do decide to stay. What about Tony?'

'Tony has booked two weeks' holiday from work. Whether he decides to remain here or go back after that time is up to him. I can't say what he'll do.'

'Are you telling me that you haven't discussed it?'

Alice lifted her shoulders. 'No. I'm saying he hasn't reached a decision.'

'I see. There's one thing I think you should bear in mind, Alice. This is my house, and Tony is not welcome here. He can remain for his two weeks, but after that I want him out, whether he's your fiancé or not.'

'I'll tell him,' she said quietly. 'Now would you mind going and letting me get changed?'

It did not take her long, but as she passed Tony's door on her way downstairs it opened and he grabbed her arm. 'What was Jared doing in your room?' he demanded angrily.

Alice could not disguise her surprise. 'How did you know?'

'I was coming to see you myself and heard voices. What did he want?'

'To tell me that dinner was almost ready,' she said.

'And the rest!' he snarled. 'He was in there for over five minutes.'

'So you timed us?' she demanded.

'No, I did not,' he said with exaggerated patience. 'But I think I have a right to know what was going on.'

'If you must know, we were making love.'

His eyes widened with shock. 'Alice! How could you? Of all the——'

She laughed and put her fingers to his mouth. 'Tony, for heaven's sake, all we were doing was talking! Do you really think I'd let him do that?'

He lifted his shoulders. 'I don't know what to think. I feel there's more to it than you're admitting. Your reaction yesterday when we arrived was so strong, you looked as though you'd seen a ghost. Something happened between you, didn't it, when he was in England?'

'Don't talk rubbish,' she said sharply. 'Jared came over to check that we were all right, because my grandfather asked him to, that's all. As for anything happening—well, that's preposterous. He spent more time with my mother than me. I was only sixteen, for heaven's sake!'

Tony nodded, though he didn't look satisfied. 'You still haven't told me what you were talking about just now.'

He was persistent, if nothing else. 'I don't see that I

have to answer to you for everything I do,' she said irately. 'But if it will make your mind easier, he wanted to know whether I'd reached a decision about staying.'

'And he had to come to your bedroom to ask you that?'

Alice swung away. Questions, questions, all these questions. Anyone would think he was her minder! 'Go to hell, Tony,' she said crossly.

'But, Alice, all I'm trying to do is——'

He was cut short by the appearance of Jared. 'A lovers' tiff already?'

Tony glared. 'It has nothing to do with you.'

'But you are guests in my house, and I don't care to hear raised voices. If you're ready, Alice.' And Jared took her arm and led her downstairs.

She tried to struggle free, but his grip was fierce. Tony followed, his footsteps heavy at their heels. He sat opposite her at the dining table, his face red with rage.

'I wonder what delicacies Mrs Bell has provided for us tonight,' said Jared, smiling at them both as if nothing had happened. 'She really is an excellent cook.'

'What the hell's going on between you and Alice?' demanded Tony loudly.

Jared's brows rose and he looked at Tony smoothly. 'Going on? Between me and Alice? If there is something then I'm as much in the dark as you. Alice what have you been saying to this boy?'

Alice stifled a giggle. Tony was not amused by Jared sending him up, but his outrage was even more ridiculous.

'I know you were in her room. I want to know——'

'Tony,' cut in Alice, 'I think you should shut up and stop making an ass of yourself. I told you what Jared wanted.'

'And I don't believe you,' he snarled. 'If you want to be together then please carry on, I'm getting out of here.' He glared at them both and scraping back his chair left the room.

'Poor Tony,' said Jared. 'He is in a state.'

'You're not helping!' snapped Alice.

'He shouldn't have come.'

'I needed someone.'

'Would you have needed someone if you'd known I'd be here?' There was an amused gleam in his eyes.

'More than ever,' Alice said savagely.

'Am I such an ogre?'

'You're——' How could she put it? 'You belong to a part of my life that I'd prefer to forget, which I had forgotten until I saw you again. Why did you have to be here?' It was a desperate cry.

'I promised Daniel that I'd look after you.'

Her head jerked. 'So you did know about the letter? You did know he was going to ask me to live here?'

He nodded.

'So why didn't you tell me?' she accused harshly. 'It was such a shock! I can't possibly stay, you do know that?'

Jared's mouth became grim all of a sudden, his eyes hardening. 'Your grandfather loved you, Alice, even though he'd never met you. When I came back after seeing you and your mother he made me tell him every minute detail. He couldn't hear enough about you. You were his only grandchild, you and Gillian the only family he had.'

She eyed him scornfully. 'It was his fault. He deserved to be unhappy. He said something in his letter about writing to my mother, but it's the first I've heard of it and I'm afraid I don't believe him. No!' She shook her head vigorously. 'From what I've heard about my grandfather it's a good job we never met. I couldn't have been civil to him. He destroyed my mother. Her whole life was one long, uphill struggle, and I'll never forgive him, ever!'

Her protest left Jared unmoved. 'You can say what you like, Alice, Daniel wanted to love you, he really did. He was denied it in his lifetime. Are you now going to deny him his dying wishes?'

She met his eyes bravely. 'He evidently didn't know what he was asking. I suppose you didn't tell him about—about what happened between you and me in England? If you had he would have realised how impossible such an arrangement is.'

'I don't find the situation impossible,' he annouced smoothly.

'But I do,' she gritted. 'I can't possibly stay here with you. Besides, what would I do for three months?'

'I'm sure you'll find some way of amusing yourself,' he mocked cheerfully.

'And how about clothes? I've brought only enough for a few days.'

'You can buy some.'

'What with?' she demanded scornfully.

'Certainly not with what Dan left for your holiday. I don't think he thought about clothes. But you could allow me to treat you.'

She eyed him thoughtfully. 'Tell me, Mr Jared Clever Duvall, do you know what I'll come into—if I do stay? Is that why you're being so generous? Are you confident of getting it all back? Or is it perphaps your conscience that's bothering you? You and your son between you have taken so much of my grandfather's estate that buying me a few clothes is the least you can do?'

'Leave my son out of this!' he snarled, his face contorting furiously. 'And no, I don't know what Dan's left you. Though if you ask me you deserve nothing. I find it very hard to believe that you've gone through the whole of your life without ever once trying to contact him. It broke his heart, do you know that? And just for the record, I have not taken one cent of Daniel's money. This house was bought at a fair price. And whatever he's left for Luke was Daniel's own doing. I knew nothing about it until after his death.'

'I think you do know what I'll get,' Alice said tersely. 'My grandfather probably swore you to silence.'

'Suit yourself,' he shrugged.

'Did my grandfather lose absolutely everything?'

'As far as I know. Of course, he's had time to build up a fair nest-egg again.'

'Doing what?' she snapped. 'I thought he was completely ruined? How could he have started again?'

'Daniel had a shrewd business brain,' he informed her. 'He set himself up as a consultant. He grew to know these islands as well as the natives, better than most, and there were so many people wishing to go into the charter business without really knowing too much about it that he was in constant demand.'

Alice's eyes widened. 'I see. Mr Lewis never told me that.'

'There was no reason why he should,' shrugged Jared. 'He told me everything else.'

'He told you what he thought you should know.'

'So why have you told me that my grandfather had some money to leave after all?'

'Because I thought it might help you make up your mind.'

Her eyes widened. 'You want me to stay?' And her pulses began to race.

But there was no warmth on his face when he spoke. 'If I were your grandfather I wouldn't have left you anything. I would have treated you with the contempt you deserve.'

Alice gasped.

'How you and your mother could treat him so shabbily I'll never know,' Jared added.

'I like that,' she returned sharply. 'You're suggesting he didn't treat us badly?

'In the beginning, yes, but as he got older he desperately

wanted his family around him.'

'Too bad!' she spat. 'There are some things that are too vile ever to put right, and turning his pregnant daughter out was one of them.'

'And now his granddaughter is going to carry on the boycott. I wonder you ever came.'

Alice eyed him coldly. 'I wasn't aware that I was given a choice. The ticket came with the command.'

'You could have sent it back.'

She raised her brows but said nothing.

'It would appear that somewhere inside you, Alice, is a mercenary streak. All your life you've wanted nothing to do with your grandfather, you still hate his guts even now he's dead, yet the thought of getting your hands on his money made you come all this way against your will.'

'Why shouldn't I receive my rightful inheritance?' she demanded.

'Rightful?' he demanded. 'Why is it that families always think they should be the automatic beneficiaries, even though there's never been any love between them?'

'I didn't ask my grandfather to leave me anything,' Alice pointed out.

'No, you didn't,' he admitted. 'Daniel was a fool.'

'And if you'd had your way I wouldn't be here now?' she demanded.

'That's right,' he said.

His answer was like a sledgehammer blow to Alice's heart. He was telling her more clearly than before that she meant nothing to him. 'That's a pity,' she returned icily, 'because I've suddenly made up my mind that I'm going to stay.' She would write to her landlord and he could sub-let the house until she got back.

There was no emotion at all on Jared's face, his eyes were blank. He looked at her for several seconds. 'In that case, Alice, we'll arrange a shopping trip for tomorrow.

Now, shall we eat?'

But Alice suddenly had no appetite for food. Too much had happened too quickly. The whole day seemed to have been taken up by discussions and arguments and hostile conversations, and she'd had enough. She needed to escape, from both of them. 'I'm not hungry,' she said. 'Please excuse me.'

She left the house and began to walk steadily and determinedly down the mountain road. She had burned her boats now; whether she liked it or not she was staying.

Three months she had, to decide whether she wanted to spend the rest of her life here. It would most probably be three months of hell, because there was no denying that her feelings for Jared were increasing by the minute, while he had made it perfectly clear that he felt nothing at all for her.

But she had no intention of changing her mind. This was something more than the dying request of an old man. It was a personal challenge. She would prove to herself, and to Jared, that he meant nothing to her. She would be friendly and polite, but a little distant, too. She would let him see by her actions and words that she had got over him. And if he should attempt to try anything, even so much as to hold her hand, she would back off so quickly that he could be in no doubt what her feelings were.

She had not been walking long when she heard her name being called and, turning, she saw Tony running after her. She felt like screaming at him to go away.

'What are you doing?' he asked, before he had even caught her up.

'I wanted to be alone,' she said pointedly.

'You didn't eat your dinner either?'

She shook her head.

'He's getting up your nose as well?'

Alice said nothing.

'He's a pretty insolent sort of bloke,' remarked Tony. 'I

don't know why we put up with him.'

'It is his house we're staying in,' she reminded him.

'Do we have to?' he asked. 'Couldn't we move into a hotel?'

'Those are the terms of my grandfather's will,' Alice said quietly.

He looked at her with a sudden frown. 'You've made up your mind?'

She nodded.

'You're staying?'

'Yes.'

Tony did not look surprised. 'Then I'll stay too. You need some one to protect you from Jared.'

'He won't let you stay on at Blue Vista,' she told him.

His chin jerked. 'You've discussed it?'

Alice nodded. 'You can stay for two weeks, but that's all. I'm sorry, Tony, but I have no say in the matter.'

His face was grim as they trudged side by side down the hill, but it did not take him long to reach his decision. 'Fair enough, I'll move out. But I'm not going home, I'm not leaving you here alone, Alice. I shall see you every day.' He stopped and turned her to him. 'I love you, don't forget. You're my girl, and the sooner Jared realises that the better!'

Alice smiled weakly. 'You're sure it's not because you think there's going to be a lot of money in the end? You're not hoping for a hand-out, are you, Tony?'

He looked hurt. 'Not you as well, Alice? Money is the last thing on my mind. Don't believe a word Jared says. It's you I'm thinking about, honestly.'

But Jared's accusations were still churning in her mind, and Alice found herself wondering if Tony were speaking the truth. The seeds of suspicion had been sown, and for the first time she doubted him.

# CHAPTER FIVE

WHEN Alice went downstairs the next morning both Jared and Tony were sitting at the breakfast table, and there was no denying which of the two men attracted her more.

Jared looked fresh and cheerful, his white shirt complementing his golden tan, his muscled chest revealed by the open top buttons. Tony, on the other hand, looked as though he hadn't slept a wink, and he had a yellow T-shirt with 'Top Dog' printed on it. Alice wondered whether he was trying to say something.

She had not had a very good night herself, and hoped there wasn't going to be another scene.

If only Jared would accept Tony, instead of continually running him down, it would make life a lot easier. She seemed to be the pig in the middle, and it was very wearing. But she put on a smile and greeted them both, and Tony got to his feet and kissed her cheek. Jared merely nodded.

'How about if I hire a car today?' suggested Tony, once they had begun to eat. 'It's about time we went exploring.'

Alice flickered a glance at Jared, saw the slight warning lift of his eyebrows. 'I'm sorry, I've already arranged to go out with Jared,' she apologised.

Tony frowned. 'Out where?' His tone was sharp.

'He's taking me shopping.'

'What for? Shouldn't that be my responsibility? I'm sure Jared has work to do.'

'Sorry Chatwin,' smiled Jared, 'but this is strictly

business. Alice needs some new clothes since she's decided to stay on.'

Tony's shock deepened. 'What's that to do with you?' he demanded.

'He's treating me,' said Alice. There was no point in keeping it a secret.

Tony's face flushed an angry red. 'I see. And when was this little party arranged?'

'At dinner last night,' she replied.

'And you didn't think to tell me?'

'I didn't know you were making plans,' she protested.

'I sure as hell don't intend hanging around here every day!'

'We'll go somewhere tomorrow,' she said, smiling, trying to lessen the hurt he must be feeling.

'Never mind tomorrow. I'd hoped to do some windsurfing later this afternoon.' Tony's lip curled in a sneer. 'You will be back?'

Alice looked at Jared, her brows arched.

'I shouldn't think so,' he said. 'I thought of making a day of it.'

Tony nearly choked. He spluttered and coughed, and when he had control of himself he said tightly, 'And where does that leave me?'

'To do what you like,' said Jared smoothly. 'Hire that car, go exploring on your own. You'll be able to tell Alice all about it tonight.'

'Thanks for nothing!' hurled Tony. 'Some holiday this is proving to be! I'm beginning to wonder exactly how much of Alice's time you intend to commandeer.'

Jared smiled evenly. 'Don't worry, you'll see plenty of Alice. Work does claim my attention sometimes.'

'I still think you should have consulted me, Alice, before agreeing,' Tony grumbled. 'I don't like him spending money on you. It's not right. Not when you're my girl.'

'Perhaps you'd like to do it yourself?' suggested Jared pleasantly.

Tony flashed him an angry glance. 'I don't have that sort of money.'

'But you'd like it?'

He lifted his shoulders. 'Who wouldn't?'

'You won't get it here.'

'Jared!' exclaimed Alice. 'Drop it, will you?'

He smiled easily. 'Touched a raw nerve, have I?'

'You're despicable!' she snapped.

'It's all right,' said Tony. 'I can take it.' He touched Alice's arm. 'You and I both know the real reason I'm here, and that's all that matters. Have a good day, Alice, and I'll see you tonight.' He squeezed her hand and left the room.

Immediately they were alone she glared at Jared. 'You had no right saying that! You've no proof he's after money and I wish you'd shut up about it.' She was already feeling guilty because she herself had doubted Tony last night.

'All right,' he agreed, shrugging expressively. 'I don't want to spoil our day arguing about him, anyway. Are you ready? I think we should go.'

Once outside, she dropped heavily into the seat of his battered sports car, folding her hands in her lap, and staring doggedly to the front .

'Aren't you elated at the thought of buying a whole new wardrobe of clothes?' Jared was smiling cheerfully, as though the conversation over breakfast had never taken place. 'Most women would give their eye-teeth to be in your place.'

'I'm not most women,' she snapped.

'It was your idea to stay.'

'I know,' she said, looking angrily into his mocking blue eyes.

'You want to change your mind?'

'No!'

He grinned. 'Then cheer up. Don't tell me you're worried about Tony? I'm sure he'll have no difficulty at all in amusing himself. There are some pretty girls on the beaches here. He'll have fun.'

'Tony wouldn't two-time me,' Alice said hotly. 'I have no qualms about that.'

'You simply don't like the thought of wearing clothes that have been paid for by me?'

She glared. 'Most definitely not!'

His lips quivered. 'You could make do with what you have. In this heat you don't need to wear much. I'd have no complaints if you went skinny-dipping or sunbathed in the nude.'

His amusement annoyed her as much as his suggestion. 'Don't be disgusting!' she snapped.

Jared's brows rose. 'I didn't realise you were a prude.'

'You're determined to make me feel uncomfortable, aren't you?' she tossed.

He smiled. 'I'm merely trying to be helpful!'

'I can do without comments like that!'

He smiled to himself as they wound down the mountainside, and Alice sat with her fingers linked tightly together. But she could not deny the feelings that were stirring inside her. Arguing with him added to her stimulation rather than detracted from it. Her whole body was vibrantly aware of him, despite the vows she had made to herself. And this was only the beginning!

There were several boutiques in St Helena and Jared seemed to know his way round them, making her wonder how many other girls he had taken shopping there.

But the clothes they sold were exciting and exotic, and she discovered that Jared had excellent taste. He seemed to know unerrringly what would suit her, and she could not argue with him. She wished she could, but she loved everything he chose. The embarrassing part was when he made her model each one in front of him.

It didn't stop there either. He took her next to a shop that sold exclusive lingerie, and he still didn't bat an eyelid, inspecting each of the delicate garments and then deciding which ones she should try on. To her relief he did not demand a fashion parade this time.

Sandals and swimwear were next added to the list, and finally they had finished. 'Lunch now, I think,' said Jared. 'I know just the place.'

'Can't we go home—I mean back to your house?' asked Alice.

He smiled at her slip. 'I'm glad you feel that way about Blue Vista—it does have a comfortable feel to it. But no, I don't think we should go back yet. I doubt if Tony will be there in any case.'

She hadn't been thinking about Tony, she simply wanted to get away from Jared. Spending so long in his company was rekindling feelings she would far rather forget. She had discovered it was not easy being distant with him.

'I'm in your hands, then,' she shrugged.

'Oh, that you were!' he mocked.

Her face flamed.

Jared laughed. 'Come on, let's go.'

It was only a short drive to the open-air restaurant which fronted a white palm-fringed beach and a crystal-clear sea that changed from palest aquamarine to deepest azure. The tables and chairs were set beneath an awning of palm leaves, and Alice gazed about her with shining wide eyes. 'I'd love to swim in that water. Is it really as warm as it looks?'

'It's like silk,' he said, 'and I can assure you you'll have plenty of time for swimming.'

Alice nodded. 'I suppose I will.'

The salad she ordered was crisp and cold, and the passionfruit juice punch Jared recommended was delicious. Alice found herself relaxing and forgetting he was her enemy.

'Have you lived here all your life?' she asked, deciding it was about time she found out more about him. 'Mr Lewis told me you were in the Bahamian police force?'

'I was born here,' he admitted, 'but my mother is English and I was educated in England.'

Which explained why he spoke English so excellently. She had thought he was English when she first met him. 'Where are your parents now?' she asked.

'They live in Eleuthera, in the Bahamas.'

'Do you go to see them?'

'Frequently. What is this, an inquisition?' Jared demanded, but he was smiling.

'You know all about me,' she said. 'Why shouldn't I find out something about you?'

'I don't know everything about you,' he said with a wry smile. 'For instance, I don't know how many boyfriends you've had since I was over there. You said you'd been in love too many times to mention. Is that true? Are you really so fickle? Was I one of many?' His eyes hardened and he watched her closely.

'Would it matter if you were?' she wanted to know.

'I don't like to think of you giving yourself freely to every Tom, Dick and Harry who shows interest.'

'You think that's what I do?'

'You virtually offered yourself to me,' he reminded her.

'I asked for a kiss!'

'You also said that you wanted me.'

'Did I?' Alice could not remember. Oh lord, she hadn't, had she? 'I know I said I loved you,' she went on. 'It was pretty stupid of me, wasn't it? I was at that impressionable age. I'm glad you didn't take me seriously.'

'And have there been others?' he insisted.

'I think that's my business,' she said. How could she tell him that she had never felt the same about anyone else? There had been dates, of course, many of them, but not one had interested her, not like Jared had.

He looked cross that she had evaded his question. 'And now there's Tony. Tell me more about him.'

'Tony is my next-door neighbour,' Alice explained impatiently. 'He's lived there for two years. We get on like a house on fire, or we did do before we came here, and I've never been to bed with him. Is that what you want to know?'

'Is that because he's never asked you, or because you refused?'

Alice gasped at his audacity. 'Tony's a gentleman!'

'Such a gentleman that he didn't decide he wanted to marry you until he discovered you might be a rich woman?'

'Is that all you can think about?' she demanded haughtily.

'Oh, no,' he grinned. 'I can think of lots of other things. Such as how I'd like to kiss you at this moment. You look so beautiful when you're angry.'

'And you have a damned cheek!' she flashed. 'Flattery won't get you anywhere.'

'Is it a crime to want to kiss a girl?'

'Not if it's for the right reasons,' she said, 'but you've made it perfectly clear that you're not interested in me, and for the record, I'm not interested in you either. I'm going to marry Tony.'

Jared let that pass. 'Are you denying that you feel anything at all?'

'No, I'm not,' she replied, knowing it was useless to lie. 'But I've learned to school my emotions. I'm not into casual sex.'

'Admirable sentiments,' he mocked, 'but not much fun, eh?'

'You think kissing me is fun?'

He grinned. 'It's not exactly the word I would use.'

'You miss having a woman around, do you?' she jeered. 'And I'll do because I happen to be here?'

Jared's smile disappeared. 'I've never denied, Alice, that I find you attractive. Even as a sixteen-year-old you had something, and if I hadn't had scruples I would have taken what you were offering.'

He paused for his words to take effect, then went on, 'And the same principles still apply. I don't play around. I have to genuinely like a person and be attracted to her, and be friends with her, before I form any sort of a relationship. And she has to feel the same way. I don't go in for one-night stands, if that's what you're insinuating.'

Did that mean he felt something for her? In a way he must do, but it certainly wasn't love, it was more likely to be because of the promise he had made her grandfather, and Alice had no intention of risking a broken heart by reviving the love she had once felt for him. It had been strictly filed away in the recesses of her mind, and for her own good it had to stay there. Tony was her defence.

'Are you stuck for words?' he taunted, when she made no response.

Alice lifted her shoulders. 'There's nothing to say. You've made your point.'

'I still want to kiss you.'

'Carry on wishing,' she crisped.

'Am I going to get no thanks at all for the clothes I bought you this morning?'

Alice felt immediately ungrateful. 'I do thank you,' she said, 'most sincerely. It was a very kind gesture. But I shall pay you back as soon as I can.'

Jared's mouth hardened. 'That wasn't why I did it.'

'I know,' she said. 'But I'd feel better.'

'If you so much as attempt it I'll be so angry you'll wonder what's hit you,' he grated. 'If you really want to repay me you can do so by being more friendly. If we're to live together for the next three months we can't go on like this.'

He was right, of course, but to relax and be herself with him would mean giving away the feelings that were churning inside her. There was no way that she could hide them. Even now her whole body was responding to his. His very masculinity was a threat.

'I'll try,' she said quietly.

Jared nodded. 'I don't suppose things will get any better until Tony's gone.'

'He's staying too,' she said quietly

Jared swore, and Alice tensed in her seat.

'Don't worry,' she said, 'he'll move out of Blue Vista in a couple of weeks.'

'But he'll still hang around. Alice, you're making a mistake if you marry that lad. He doesn't love you. Do you think he'd have let you come out with me today if he did? Believe me, he's only thinking of himself. I've seen things that you haven't. I've watched him closely. All he's concerned with is feathering his own nest.'

'No, Jared.' She shook her head firmly.

'Yes, Alice.' He took her hands across the table. 'He didn't even mention marriage, did he, until you were here and he saw for himself what sort of a life-style he could have?'

She looked down at their fingers entwined together, his so brown and firm, her own pale and delicate. 'I don't know what to think any more. What you say makes sense, but——'

'It *is* sense,' he cut in firmly. 'Think about it, Alice. Think hard. Don't get taken in by easy words. Cast your mind back. When was it he first started getting more friendly? When a casual relationship was suddenly no longer enough?'

'I suppose,' said Alice, 'that——'

'No, not now,' he said. 'Think about it when you're alone. Go over all the conversations you've had. Concentrate on Tony. And then tell me tomorrow what you've come up with.'

The day did not end there either. When they eventually got back to Blue Vista, after driving along the coast and admiring various beauty spots, Tony was not there, and when he had not returned by early evening Jared suggested they go out to dinner. 'It's obvious he's not coming,' he said. 'He's either still angry, or he's found himself a friend.'

Alice knew she ought to refuse, but she could not. He was like a drug. She had spent a whole day with him and still hadn't had enough. In fact the more she saw of him the more she wanted him, and Tony faded further and further from her mind.

'Wear your new silver dress,' said Jared softly.

Alice nodded. She had declared she would never have the opportunity to wear it, but he had insisted on buying it all the same. How like Jared to make that opportunity!

She showered and pulled on a pair of lacy white silk briefs. She had never owned silk undies before. They felt delightfully sensual against her skin.

The dress was too low-cut to wear a bra, but that did not worry her. She had acquired the faintest of tans during these last two days, carefully oiling herself so that she did not burn, and not staying in the sun too long. And it had paid off. In fact she could not remember ever having looked healthier.

She dusted her eyelids a pearly blue and thickened her lashes with mascara, but that was all the make-up she used before stepping into the silvery-white creation.

For once she swept her hair up, pinning it with glittering combs also bought that day, and fixing long crystal earrings into her ears. They looked like tear-drops. Jared had given them to her when they got home. 'They belonged to Mary,' he told her. 'Dan bought them for her. I know he'd like you to have them.'

They had looked so fragile and lovely in their blue satin box, and although she felt she ought to refuse, Alice had picked them up and held them against her face and fallen immediately in love with them.

When she got downstairs Jared was waiting for her. She felt like a princess in the shimmering dress that skimmed her curves and flared around her knees, and with the silver high-heeled sandals she knew she looked like a million dollars.

Jared looked good too in a white jacket and a silk shirt with a navy bow tie. In fact he looked so devastating that her heart flipped and every nerve-end felt as though it had been set on fire.

He held out his hands to her and she walked towards him, smiling. But Jared did not touch her as she wanted him to. His arms fell to his sides as she reached him, although their eyes met and held and Alice's thoughts winged back six years. 'I love you, Jared,' she had said then, and despite everything the words were still true today. Exactly what, she wondered, had she let herself in for?

Tonight it was no battered sports car but a sleek grey limousine that smelled of leather and Jared's aftershave, and as he handed her into it his arm brushed her breast.

Alice held her breath and closed her eyes. Was it deliberate? Did he know she was wearing nothing underneath? Did he know what feelings such an action would evoke? But when she opened them again he was sitting beside her and inserting his key into the ignition, and not even looking in her direction.

Inhaling deeply, Alice settled into her seat and silently lectured herself. Reacting to Jared like this was no good at all. The whole object of the excercise was to show him that she didn't care, and here she was behaving in exactly the same manner as she had six years ago.

'Where are we going?' she asked, and her voice came out in a squeak.

He looked across and smiled and she knew he was aware of her agitation. 'A place you'll like. A nightclub, with floor shows, and a casino in case you're feeling lucky. With a room where they play nothing but soft music and you can dance till dawn or just sit and relax and talk about whatever comes into your head. It caters for all tastes and all moods and in my opinion is one of the finest places in the islands.'

And he had not exaggerated. It was a magical, exhilarating place, where the food was superb, and Jared was a perfect companion. It was an out-of-this-world place, and Alice's eyes were wide and there was bright colour in her cheeks. She kept looking about her, taking it all in, wishing her mother could have enjoyed it with her. It was unfair that Daniel Alexander had lived so well while his daughter had had to count every penny.

'What's wrong?' Jared caught the shadow in her eyes.

'I was thinking about my mother. She would have liked it here.'

His mouth firmed. 'She could have come any time she liked.'

'She had her pride.'

'Too much of it.'

Her eyes flashed. 'You're saying that——'

Jared silenced her by reaching across the table and taking her hand. 'Let's not spoil tonight.'

She snatched free. 'I can't help it. He had so much, and—we——'

'I know,' he cut in softly. 'Believe me, I know. But Dan isn't entirely to blame.'

'Of course you'd say that,' she crisped. 'You were his friend. But you've no idea what it was like. Take all this, for instance—you'll probably spend more tonight than mother had to last her a month.' She compressed her lips and shook her head angrily. 'It's so unfair!'

Jared's eyes narrowed warningly. 'Alice, if you're going to spend the whole night comparing your life in England to this then we might as well leave. There's no comparison, I'm well aware of that. I thought you'd enjoy it.'

'I am,' she insisted. 'It's just that——' She tailed off and shook her head. 'It's so unreal.'

'You could easily get used to it,' he said.

'You mean that if I stayed here and collected my inheritance then this is the sort of life-style I would adopt?'

'Oh, no,' said Jared firmly. 'Tonight is special. Life will be humdrum after this.'

Humdrum—at Blue Vista? 'I don't think so,' she said. 'Just living in the house is like being on holiday.'

'It will pall after a while,' he assured her. 'Especially when Tony moves out.' He watched closely for her reaction.

'I shall still see him,' she said firmly.

'Of course.'

'But you could be right. Three months doing nothing isn't my idea of fun. I suppose I could always find myself a job.' It was not so much the money—she knew her grandfather had seen to it that she would not be short during her stay here—it would be the boredom.

Jared nodded his agreement. 'Let me know when you're ready. The hotels here are often on the lookout for good hairdressers. I can put in a word for you.'

After their meal they watched a dance spectacular, and then Jared took her to the casino and she tried her hand at roulette, but she did not win. Then they moved into the ballroom, and he took her into his arms and she melted against him.

The music was dreamy and hypnotic, and Alice closed her eyes and pretended Jared was in love with her. His hands held her close, his fingers caressing the smooth skin of her back, and it was so easy to forget all the bad things and remember only the good.

Suddenly she did not want the evening to end. And he must have felt her relaxing, because he said, 'Are you enjoying yourself, Alice?'

She smiled and nodded and her face was soft.

'You look absolutely beautiful. Can I take some of the credit?'

He could take all of it, if only he knew. 'I think so,' she whispered.

Jared touched his lips to her temple and his arms tightened about her, and she wanted more than just a token kiss. But it was all she got, and soon after that he suggested they go home.

In his car Alice closed her eyes and drifted on the edge of slumber. She clung to him as they walked into the house, half drugged from tiredness, very slightly inebriated from the quantity of wine she had drunk. She was conscious of smiling inanely and she felt supremely happy.

'Alice.' Jared turned her to him in the hall, and she looked up, her eyes shining. Then he shook his head. 'It doesn't matter.' Whatever he had been going to say, he had changed his mind.

'Goodnight, Jared,' she said, swallowing her disappointment, and climbed wearily up the stairs. She had thought for one moment that he was going to whisper words of love. How foolish she was! He had taken her out tonight because Tony was away and it was a fitting end to the day. But there was no more to it than that, and she would be wise to remember it.

She hung her beautiful dress away carefully, then collapsed into bed and fell immediately asleep. When she got up the next morning she discovered that Jared had already left the house.

Tony, however, was waiting for her in the breakfast room, and he did not look happy. 'Have a good day?' he demanded.

Alice shrugged and gave a weak smile. 'So-so.'

'Good enough that you had to make a night of it as well?'

'You were out,' she protested. 'What did you expect me to do, sit and twiddle my thumbs?'

'I came back and you weren't here, and I spent a most boring night on my own.'

'You should have come back earlier.' Alice began to feel resentful. 'Or was it because you were having too good a time? It's all right with me if you were, but just don't try and make me feel guilty.'

'Why?' jeered Tony. 'Because you were enjoying yourself too much? I knew it wouldn't be long before he won you over. I suppose you'll be seeing more of him now than you do me?'

'Don't be childish, Tony. As far as Jared's concerned I'm your girlfriend.'

'And I wonder why that little charade is necessary?' His face was contorted with disgust and anger. 'A little trick to make him want you all the more, eh? Don't deny it. I know he wants you—I've seen it in his eyes. How about you, do you want him?'

'Like I'd want a nest full of vipers,' Alice lied boldly. 'And I think this conversation's gone far enough. If you want me to go out with you today, Tony, then you'd better change your attitude and the topic of conversation, fast. Otherwise you can get out of here and go back to England, because I shan't want to see you again.'

'I'm sorry, Alice.' Pain flickered through his eyes. 'I really am. I'm jealous of Jared, you know that. I can't help it.'

'You've no need to be,' she said distantly.

'But you spent the whole day with him and didn't get in until the early hours. What was I supposed to think?'

She shrugged. 'Perhaps I'm as much to blame as you. But there really was nothing in it, Tony.' He hadn't even tried to kiss her!

'I believe you,' he said, the glimmer of a smile curving his lips. 'Let's eat, shall we, and then, if it's all right with you, we'll go windsurfing. I found a super beach yesterday. You'll love it, I know you will. I've hired a car for the whole fortnight, so we can go out whenever we like, and to hell with Jared Duvall.'

They had a hilarious time windsurfing. Alice discovered that it was more difficult keeping her balance than it looked, and she spent more time in the water than on it. Tony on the other hand had mastered the art already and found her clumsy attempts highly amusing.

They threw themsleves down on the beach afterwards. Alice closed her eyes and pulled a pained face. 'I'm totally exhausted, and my arms are killing me! I didn't realise it was such hard work.'

'Wait till tomorrow,' warned Tony. 'You won't be able to lift them.'

'Thanks,' she groaned, opening one eye and looking at him. 'That's all I want to know!'

'The answer is to do it all over again. Is it a date?'

Alice nodded.

He leaned over and kissed her mouth, and she sat up sharply. 'Don't do that!'

'What's a kiss?' he frowned.

'Coming from you, quite a lot.'

He scowled angrily. 'You still think all I'm after is your grandfather's fortune?'

'Well, aren't you?' she demanded. 'I've been giving it some thought, and it wasn't until I showed you Mr Lewis's letter about my grandfather's death that you started getting more friendly.'

'Nonsense,' he said, though he did not quite look her in the eye.

'You were most insistent on coming out here with me, and I did think it strange, though I was so relieved to have company that I didn't pay too much attention to it at the time.'

'And rightly so,' he said. 'You're imagining things.'

'And then when we got here and you saw Blue Vista, and Perle Island, and the sort of life you could lead as my husband, you suddenly decided you were in love with me and wanted to marry me.'

'Alice!' This time he did face her and he looked genuinely hurt by what she had said. 'You're way off the mark. I've loved you for a long time. Didn't I prove it by always being there when you needed me after your mother died? I never said how I felt because you never showed any signs of returning my love. I was prepared to wait and hope and make myself indispensable, until one day you'd realise you couldn't face life without me. Then Jared forced my hand, as I've already explained, and I had to admit my feelings.'

'Is that true?' she asked quietly.

'Of course it's true,' he frowned, looking offended.

'I wish you'd told me all that before.'

'I have tried,' he said.

'You can't blame Jared for being suspicious,' said Alice reasonably. 'He doesn't know you like I do.'

'But he did a very good job of turning you round to his way of thinking.'

She nodded guiltily. 'I'm sorry.'

'I'm sorry too,' said Tony, then he took her hands into his. 'Are we still friends?'

Again Alice nodded.

He pulled her to him and kissed her, and this time she did not pull away. But his kiss meant nothing, nothing at all. He never would have that effect on her. Not that he seemed to notice it. The kiss deepened and his arms slid about her, and Alice suffered his embrace because she did not want to hurt him any more.

She had been wrong to doubt him, she realised that now. But she would never love him or marry him, and she had to make sure he knew that. Gently she pulled away. 'Tony, I'm sorry,' she said gently.

He put his fingers to her lips. 'Don't say it—I know. But let's just go along as we are, mm?'

And she hadn't the heart to say no.

They sat for a while watching the surfers, then suddenly Tony said, 'I wish you hadn't let that man spend money on you.'

Alice had not even been aware that his thoughts were running in that direction and his statement was quite a shock. 'I thought it was a very kind gesture,' she defended.

'Kind, my foot!' snarled Tony. 'He wouldn't do it without a motive.'

'So what am I supposed to wear for the next three months? I haven't that kind of money. Even my grandfather's allowance doesn't take clothes into account.'

'Hell, I don't know, do I? But I do know that you shouldn't have accepted charity from him. It's enough that you have to live in the same house.'

'What do you propose I do, then?' demanded Alice. 'Go back to England and forget about my inheritance?'

'Good lord, no!'

His answer was too quick and too vehement, and Alice looked at him sharply.

But his smile was reassuring. 'You deserve it,' he said. 'Every penny.'

'Actually,' she said. 'I'm not sure now that I'm doing the right thing. I sometimes wish I hadn't come. I don't want people to think that I'm a gold-digger.'

'For pity's sake, Alice, your grandfather wanted you to have something. Don't be stupid!'

'But I've never met him, I don't even like him. I hate his guts, if the truth's known. It's wrong, all wrong,' she sighed.

'So why did you come?'

'I don't know,' she said sadly. 'I didn't seem to have much choice. But now I wish I hadn't bothered.'

Tony was silent for a moment, then he said, 'Has this anything to do with Jared Duvall?'

Alice felt the blood creeping into her cheeks and there was no way she could hide it. 'I suppose so,' she admitted.

'Exactly what's going on between you two? You said he was a friend of your mother, but it strikes me that there's more to it than that. What happened when he was in England?'

Alice smiled mirthlessly. 'Nothing really. We just didn't see eye to eye.'

'And now?'

She lifted her shoulders in a helpless gesture. 'I don't know.' The sun was burning her back and she pulled her towel more closely about her.

'He's being a nuisance?' Tony persisted. 'That's why you want to leave?'

'No!' she protested. 'It's not like that. I just don't feel comfortable with him.' Jared was being kind to her for Daniel's sake, but in reality he despised her for denying her grandfather's existence. And it hurt. She didn't care about the money, she really didn't. It was Jared who was keeping her here.

'Has he kissed you again? Has he tried to make love to you?'

She shook her head.

Tony looked relieved. 'In that case I think you're worrying for nothing. He's obviously realised he can't get anywhere with you. I can't say I blame him for trying it on; what man wouldn't? You're a real beauty, Alice. I think you'll find after a few days that things will settle down and he'll carry on with his work and leave you alone.'

'He's going to get me a job,' she told him.

Again he looked astonished. 'What sort of a job?'

'Hairdressing, at one of the hotels.'

'But why the hell do you want to work? Was it his idea or yours?'

'Mine,' she confirmed. 'I can't sit around for three months doing nothing. What have you got against it?'

'Nothing,' Tony shrugged. 'It's just that that man seems to be organising your entire life.'

Alice pushed herself up. 'I think it's time we went back to Blue Vista,' she decided.

Instantly he was contrite. 'Oh, please, not yet. Let's go and have a drink and a bite to eat.'

Reluctantly Alice agreed, and they pulled on some clothes and made their way to a nearby hotel. They sat in the beautifully cool and airy lounge for a while and she sipped Campari and soda and listend to Tony talking without taking anything in.

After several minutes she came aware of someone watching her. It was a strange feeling, a prickly sensation riding down on her spine, and she turned her head—and encountered Jared Duvall's stony gaze.

Her heart jolted. What was he doing here? It was a pointless question. It was obvious: he was keeping an eye on them. She glared angrily and turned her attention back to Tony.

He caught the glint of fury and frowned and followed the direction her eyes had taken. 'What's he doing here?' he hissed, unconsciously reiterating her own question.

'Your guess is as good as mine,' she replied, her tone hard.

'He followed us?'

Alice shook her head. 'He couldn't have done. He'd already gone out when we left.'

'He disapproves of me, I know that, but this is beyond a joke!' Tony stood up. 'I'm going to have a word with him.'

'Tony, no!' But she was too late, he was already striding across the room.

# CHAPTER SIX

ALICE could not hear what Jared and Tony were saying, but it was clear by their expressions and the aggressive line of their bodies that they were arguing.

When Tony came back his face was red. 'Damn that man! He wants to know why we think he should want to spy on us.'

'You actually said we thought he was spying?' asked Alice incredulously.

'What the hell else is he doing? He's made it very obvious that he doesn't approve of our friendship. I still think he fancies you, no matter what you say, and I think he's just keeping an eye on us, ready to jump in if I make a wrong move.'

'You're overreacting,' said Alice, even though she did wonder why Jared was sitting there watching them when he should have been at the office.

'Am I?' demanded Tony belligerently. 'I don't think so. Let's get out of here. I don't want to sit and eat with him breathing down our necks. And if he dares follow I'll stick my fist in his face!'

Alice said nothing, though she could not resist glancing at Jared as they walked from the lounge. He looked far from pleased. But when he beckoned her to him she wished she hadn't turned her head. Tony had stalked on ahead and was already out of the doors, and she hesitated a second before crossing to Jared's side.

'You can tell that fancy boyfriend of yours,' he said without preamble, 'to get himself out of my house. He's not welcome there any longer.'

'Jared,' she protested, 'I'm sure he didn't mean what he said. He was just a little uptight, that's all.'

'A little? I'm too much of a gentleman to repeat what he said, Alice, but I didn't like it, and I don't want to see him again. Is that clear?'

His tone brooked no argument. She nodded. 'I'm sorry if he upset you, but he did it for my sake. He saw I wasn't pleased to see you here and——'

'And why was that, may I ask?' Jared demanded coldly.

'You made me feel uncomfortable, sitting here watching us, and although I didn't want Tony to say anything to you, I——'

'You didn't attempt to stop him?' he asked scathingly. 'What do you take me for? Why do you think I'd want to spy on you? I don't like Chatwin, I've made that perfectly clear, but what you and he do is no business of mine.' He paused a moment, then said, 'Don't forget to relay my message.' And Alice was dismissed.

When she got outside Tony was standing impatiently on the steps. 'What kept you?' he wanted to know.

'I had a word with Jared.'

'You did what?' he frowned. 'I hope you weren't apologising?'

Alice shook her head. 'What do you take me for? Come on, let's go back home. I'll tell you on the way.' She knew that if she told him now he would go back inside and there would be an unholy row.

And his reaction when she did finally convey Jared's message proved that she had been right to wait.

'He can't do this to me—I won't go!' he shouted, his face turning its usual blustering red. 'Alice, I hope you told him he was being unreasonable?'

She eyed him worriedly. 'Jared was in no mood to listen to anything I wanted to say. He's really angry, Tony. If I were you I'd do as he says. He could make your life very difficult.'

'As if he hasn't already!'

'But it is his house. He has every right.'

'Are you sticking up for him?'

'Of course not,' she said swiftly. 'Though I didn't want you to speak to him in the first place. I wish you weren't so hot-tempered.'

'How can I help it, the way he treats me?' snarled Tony.

When they arrived back at Blue Vista he began to pack his belongings, while Alice found Mrs Bell and asked her to make them some lunch. They sat out on the terrace eating it and there was an air of gloom over them.

'I'm only going for your sake,' said Tony after a while. 'I don't want to cause any unpleasantness—he might take it out on you. But I want you to promise you'll see me every day. I'll be bored out of my mind if you don't. I'll come here and pick you up as soon as he's gone to work and we can go windsurfing or whatever, and it need make no difference, need it?'

He seemed to want her reassurance, and Alice nodded. 'None at all.'

'And you will keep your distance from Jared?'

That was one thing she fully intended doing. She had to, for her own peace of mind.

Tony lingered long after their meal was finished, and in the end Alice had to persuade him to go. She was afraid of Jared coming home early and finding him here, and she did not feel up to another scene.

But the house felt very empty afterwards and she wandered around aimlessly for what seemed like hours, until suddenly Jared turned up. She was sitting on the terrace, and he dropped down into one of the vacant cane chairs.

'Has Tony gone?' he asked.

Alice nodded. 'He wasn't very happy about it.'

'He has only himself to blame.'

'You didn't have to be so hard on him.'

Jared smiled. 'Actually he gave me the excuse I was looking for. He should never have come. It wasn't what your grandfather wanted at all.'

Alice eyed him coldly. 'Don't pass the buck. It wasn't what you wanted, and you know it.'

'OK,' he admitted, much to her surprise. 'Me as well. But I blame you. You should have asked before bringing him. The single air ticket should have told you you were expected alone.'

'And you know that I'm not used to travelling. My mother and I hardly ever went anywhere.'

'Your grandfather imagined you were adult enough now to make the journey without someone holding your hand.'

'Then he was wrong, wasn't he?' demanded Alice aggressively. 'I don't regret bringing Tony, not one little bit.'

Jared's brows rose. 'I take it you've not yet given any thought to our conversation of yesterday.'

'Oh, yes, I've thought about it a lot,' she returned quickly, 'and I've decided that you're wrong and Tony has no ulterior motives at all.'

His jaw tensed and his eyes flashed. 'God, you're a fool!'

'I don't think so,' she said quietly.

'You still intend marrying him?' he growed. 'He doesn't love you, you know that? He's after ony one damn thing.'

'I don't think so,' said Alice again. 'You've no proof of it. If I went back to England tomorrow and gave up any chance at all of inheriting whatever my grandfather's left, he'd still marry me.'

He shook his head in disbelief. 'You're not only a fool, you're a gullible fool. Lord knows what line he's been spinning you, but you need your head examining if you believe he loves you.'

'I think he does,' said Alice haughtily, at the same time pushing herself to her feet. This conversation had gone far enough.

'Where are you going?' demanded Jared, reaching out and grabbing her wrist as she walked past him.

'To my room.'

His fingers tightened., 'In the middle of a conversation?'

'You wanted to know whether Tony had left and I said yes. There's nothing else to discuss.'

'I think there is,' he said quietly, and pulled her closer to him.

Alice tried to ignore her erratic pulses. 'Such as?'

'What you're going to do now?'

'Isn't that obvious?' she demanded. 'Just because Tony's not living here it doesn't mean I shall stop seeing him.'

'That's a pity,' he said. 'I was hoping you'd see more of me.'

Her heart joined her pulses on their mad excursion. 'I don't see how that's possible when you're at work every day. Besides, I wouldn't really want to.'

'No?' Jared sat forward on the edge of his seat and caught her other wrist, pulling her down until she was on her knees in front of him. 'I don't think you mean that, Alice. I think you'd very much like to spend time with me. Why are you afraid of showing your feelings? I can remember when you had no such fears.'

And so could she, and look what had happened. 'I've told you,' she said with as much dignity as she could muster from her ignoble position, 'I have no intention of giving in to sexual desires.'

'You think your body's all I'm after?'

'Well, isn't it?' she taunted.

'I could take you any time I wanted,' he said confidently. 'That's not what it's all about.'

'Then what are you trying to do?'

'I don't deny that I find you attractive,' he said. 'Nor do I deny that I'd like to make love to you. But first and foremost I think we should be friends. I said that to you yesterday, have you forgotten?'

Alice shook her head.

'You're not trying very hard.'

'Is that surprising?'

'Tony got what was coming to him,' Jared continued.

'In your eyes only.'

'I did what Daniel would have wanted me to do.'

'Daniel!' she fumed. 'I'm sick and fed up of hearing about Daniel. I don't care about him. I wish I hadn't come.'

'Do you, Alice?' He looked at her intently, and his eyes had never seemed bluer. 'I'm glad he can't hear you. He was always talking about what he would do if you did come, where he'd take you, what he'd show you, what you'd do together.'

'Did he talk about my mother as well?'

'Naturally. He spoke about both of you, often.'

'And yet he never bothered to come and see us.'

'I think he was afraid,' Jared told her.

Alice frowned. 'Of what?'

'Of his reception.'

'And he had every right to be,' she answered strongly. 'I'm glad I never saw him, do you hear? Glad!'

'Oh, Alice, how it hurts me to hear you say that,' he sighed. 'If you had known Daniel as well as I such thoughts would never enter your mind.'

'I'll never know him, will I?' she said. 'And that was his loss, not mine. He had no one but himself to blame. Please don't try to tell me what he was like, because I'll only believe what's been proved to me over the years.'

Jared's eyes darkened with anger and his fingers gripped her wrists even more tightly, digging into her soft flesh, hurting her, making her want to cry out, but she refused to give him the satisfaction.

She held his gaze boldly, but even so was not ready when his mouth claimed hers. He freed he wrists now, reaching behind her instead and imprisoning her in the circle of his arms. The hunger that had gnawed at Alice all yesterday suddenly surfaced and her body became a mass of sensation.

There was no gentleness in his kiss. She had angered him and this was his method of punishing her. The kiss was brutal in its intensity, grinding her lips back against her teeth. And when she tried to protest his kiss deepened, his tongue plundering the moistness of her mouth.

'Jared . . .' she managed a second time, but still he ignored her.

And then suddenly there was a subtle change. His kiss gentled, while at the same time it had a far more devastating effect. His mouth moved on hers with an expertise that could not be denied, drawing out an unwitting response.

A soft moan escaped her throat and she relaxed in his arms, and he groaned and gathered her closer. Now Alice drank from his mouth, parting her lips eagerly. Nothing had changed. She needed and wanted Jared as much as she ever had. Her heart pounded like a mad thing within her breast and she pressed herself even closer, swallowing his kisses, breathing her own love into him.

When his hand slid beneath her short sun-top to cup the fullness of her breast she ached with an agony of longing, and when his fingers found her nipple and played with it until it hardened, her excitement knew no bounds.

He did likewise with her other breast, and Alice let her

head sink back in sheer delirium, her lips parted, her eyes closed, tiny animal sounds of hunger coming from the back of her throat.

When Jared popped the buttons on her top and slid it gently back over her shoulders, exposing her naked breasts to his devouring eyes she could ony arch herself even closer towards him.

And when he took her nipples one by one into his mouth her head swam with sensation, her whole body a wanton primitive mass. 'Oh, Jared!' She mouthed the words without even knowing it.

'You're beautiful, Alice.' He looked at her, and touched her, and kissed her, and she watched him, loving him and aching for him, yet faintly realising the futility behind it all.

'Let's go indoors,' he groaned, covering her up again. They rose as one and with his arm about her shoulders they walked into the house.

Alice felt as though she were in a trance, and she wanted Jared as much as he wanted her. It was unfortunate that they bumped into Mrs Bell, who wanted to know how many there would be for dinner.

'Ah sure do wish someone would tell me what's going on,' she grumbled.

'Chatwin's left for good,' said Jared pleasantly. 'There'll be just me and Miss Alice.'

The woman's eyes looked over the two of them and she smiled. Jared had not removed his arm, and Alice felt the colour steal into her cheeks. She knew exactly what the housekeeper was thinking, and she wondered how many other girls he had entertained in such a manner. The fact that Mrs Bell did not look shocked made her think there must have been many.

She pulled free and ran up the stairs before Jared could stop her, making straight for her room and locking the door. To her chagrin he did not come pounding on it.

With her eyes closed she leaned against the cool wood, her heart leaping about inside her ribcage as though it would like to break free. Thank goodness for Mrs Bell's timely appearance! She trembled to think what might have happened.

It was an age before she finally came back down to earth, and even then she refused to leave her room until it was time for dinner. She hated the thought of facing Jared; she had given away far too much.

He looked at her closely as she entered the room, but she had determinedly schooled her expression and there was nothing on her face now to say that she had come close to letting him make love to her.

There was silence as they began their meal, then he said, 'Well, Alice?'

She pretended to misunderstand. 'Well what?'

'Don't play games with me,' he rasped quickly. 'Why did you rush away?'

She gazed at him frankly then. It was futile trying to avoid his questions. 'Because it was wrong.'

His brows rose. 'Wrong, feeling as we did?'

Alice nodded.

'Tell me why?'

'I'm not here to have an affair with you, Jared. I wish you'd leave me alone.'

'Do you?' His eyes darkened and there was a whole host of meaning in their depths. 'I think you're lying. I think you want me as much as I want you.'

'You're forgetting Tony,' she protested.

'Ah, yes Tony. I wonder if you respond to him as you do to me? Somehow I doubt it.'

How right he was, but it was unwise to give way to carnal desires. She had never felt like this with any other man and knew she never would, but, even so, an affair was not the answer.

Jared smiled mockingly. 'I think marrying Tony will be the biggest mistake of your life,' he told her.

'You're wrong!' she spat. 'But should it not work out, it will be my mistake and nothing at all to do with you.'

'And you're wrong there,' he corrrected firmly. 'If you marry Tony and he gets his hands on Dan's inheritance, then that's very much my business. Dan was the closest friend I've ever had, and I consider it my duty to protect his interests.'

'And you think the best way of doing it is to make me fall for you instead of Tony?' she fended hostilely.

'It's certainly one solution.'

Also proof that his interest in her was as cold-blooded as he suggested Tony's was.

'Not one that appeals to me,' she managed to reply.

'You're not a very convincing liar,' he said softly.

'I must admit I was flattered by the attention you paid me when you came to England,' she said. 'None of my mother's other friends had ever done that, and I suppose it went to my head. But there were no lasting feelings. I realised that as soon as you'd gone. Indeed, I was grateful to you for showing me how foolish I was.'

'Is that so?' His eyes narrowed disbelievingly.

'Nor will it work, me staying here with you.'

Something flickered in his eyes. 'I think we both owe it to Daniel to make sure it does. He dearly wanted you to love this place the same as he did. He still thought of it as his even after I'd bought it from him.'

'But it can never be mine, so what's the point in me staying here?' she snapped. 'Why can't I move into a hotel?'

'With Tony?' he snarled. 'Is that what this is all about?'

'Even if Tony hadn't come it would never have worked,' she said. 'Can't you see what an impossible situation my grandfather's put me in? It might have been best if you'd told him what happened between us, then he'd never have asked me to come here.'

Jared's lips twitched. 'I somehow don't think it would have made any difference. He was determined to get you here.'

'And he thought the offer of money would do the trick?' she snapped.

'He wasn't wrong. Though I guess it didn't occur to him that there might be a third party who'd show even more interest.'

Alice scraped back her chair. 'I've had enough! All you ever do is sling insults!'

'I speak the truth as I see it. Sit down, Alice, stop being childish.'

She eyed him resentfully. 'There you go again! When are you going to realise that I'm an adult and I know exactly what I'm doing?'

'When you prove it to me,' he snarled.

'And exactly how am I supposed to do that?' She gripped the back of the chair so tightly that her knuckles shone white. 'If you'd stop harassing me it might help.'

'I thought I was helping,' he said. 'At least that was my intention. It seemed to me as though you needed a guiding hand.'

'And that's why you kissed me? In which direction is it that you intend guiding me? No, don't bother to answer—I know what you're like. Goodnight, Jared, I'm going up to my room.'

'You haven't finished your dinner,' he said pointedly.

'I'm not hungry,' she retorted, and marched out of the room before he could say anything else.

Alice sat for hours at the window thinking of nothing else but Jared. He was doing his best to be nice to her for her grandfather's sake, but it just wasn't enough. She wanted more from him—she wanted his love—and if she couldn't have that, then there was no sense in getting involved in an affair. It would lead only to heartache.

Sleep did not come easily either when she eventually went to bed, and the next morning when she went downstairs she was relieved to discover Jared had already left.

Tony arrived at about ten and they spent a carefree day on the beach, and this time Alice managed to keep herself upright on the surfboard. The time fled.

'Do you have to go back?' he asked when she began to talk about returning to Blue Vista. 'Can't you stay and have dinner with me in my hotel?'

'I've already told Mrs Bell I'll be back,' she said. 'Perhaps another night?'

He looked disgruntled. 'Are you sure it's not Jared who's the attraction?'

Alice groaned inwardly. All day she had steered the conversation away from Jared. Why did he have to bring him up now?

'I'm his guest, don't forget. I can't come and go as I please. I do have to conform in some ways.'

'You will see me tomorrow?'

'Of course,' she reassured him.

The next few days followed the same pattern, her days spent with Tony, her evenings with Jared. Jared did not attempt to kiss her again, but there was no denying the chemistry that flared between them, and it was hard sitting with him, talking to him, desperately wanting him, but trying not to show it in her eyes.

And then one evening Jared announced that he had found her a job. 'The Whitesands is looking for a hairdresser,' he said. 'I've recommended you and you're to start in the morning.'

'Without them seeing me?'

He nodded. 'My word was enough.'

Alice thought he was mad. 'Even you don't know how good I am,' she pointed out.

'I have faith in you,' he said.

She felt flattered.

After dinner she rang Tony, but he wasn't in his hotel room and the receptionist had no idea when he would be back. Alice tried several more times but in the end gave up, deciding to catch him first thing in the morning.

And this time she was successful. 'I won't be able to go windsurfing with you today,' she told him. 'I've got a job.'

'You're crazy!' he exclaimed. 'I thought you'd given up that idea. What am I going to do with myself now?'

'You've made friends, go out with them,' she said gently. There was a whole crowd whom they met regularly at the beach. Tony certainly wouldn't be lonely.

'But they're not you,' he grumbled. 'Really, Alice, you're being very inconsiderate!'

At that moment Jared's hand touched her shoulder. 'If you don't hurry you're going to be late.'

'I'm sorry, Tony,' she said quickly, 'I have to go.'

'Was that Jared?' he demanded, his tone suspicious.

'Yes,' she admitted, 'he's giving me a lift. I'll ring you tonight. Bye.'

'I take it Chatwin wasn't pleased?' asked Jared as they walked into the breakfast room.

'You were listening?' she demanded.

'I couldn't help overhearing as I came downstairs,' he replied pleasantly.

'Is there no privacy in this house?'

He grinned. 'It all depends on what you're doing!'

Alice's eyes flashed, but she did not rise to the bait. 'To answer your question, no, Tony wasn't pleased.'

'He thinks working is beneath you now you're virtually a rich woman?'

'It's not that. I'm the only friend he has.'

'I doubt it,' said Jared coolly. 'But,' he added, 'you'd better make sure that worrying about him doesn't affect your work. I really laid it on thick about how good you were.'

'It won't,' she confirmed as she bit into her roll.

They hurried their breakfast and then went outside to his car. The ride down the moutainside was agonising. In the house Alice had been able to put some degree of distance between them, but in the intimacy of Jared's car there was no escape.

With every breath she drew she was filling herself with his presence. Every time he changed gear his hand came dangrously close to her thigh. She could smell his musky aftershave, feel his masculinity, and it was torture keeping her eyes on the road instead of feeding on him.

Fortunately the journey was not long, and at the Whitesands Hotel Jared introduced her to the owner of the hairdressing salon, a dusky-skinned woman with a willowy figure and a welcoming smile and the unlikely name of Hilda. Then he left.

Alice discovered she was expected to work three mornings and two afternoons per week, and perhaps a few extra hours if the job demanded it. It sounded good to her, and the salary was excellent too, and she began work quite happily on her first client.

Half-way through the morning, though, she was absolutely astonished when Tony came into the salon. How had he found out where she was working? But she soon discovered that it was not her he had come to see.

Hilda's face lit up when he approached the desk and they spoke quietly and intimately, and Tony's hand covered hers. His back was to Alice, but she could see Hilda clearly, and there was a radiance about her that only came with being in love.

Not that Alice was jealous, far from it; so far as she was

concerned Tony could chat up any girl he liked. What was galling was the fact that he had professed to love her. He had declared himself unable to manage without her, and yet here he was quite openly carrying on an affair with another woman.

She watched closely, almost forgetting the girl whose hair she was blow-drying. Jared's warning about Tony suddenly took on a different meaning.

It was not until he was leaving the salon that he saw Alice. His jaw dropped as their eyes met, but a couple of seconds was all it took for him to regain his composure, and with a smile that could fool anyone he altered his course and came over to her.

'Alice, what a surprise! I never expected to see you here.'

'Obviously,' she said drily, and looked pointedly across to Hilda, who was watching them with a frown on her face. 'What was that you were saying about having no friends?'

'I was just fixing an appointment, that's all.'

'Don't lie to me!' she snapped. 'I saw the way you two were talking. I suppose you see her every night when you've left me?'

'Please!' His face reddened and he scuffed one toe on the floor. 'We can't talk now. What time do you finish?'

'At one, but——'

'I'll meet you outside,' he said, and before she could answer he turned and walked out.

Alice was silently fuming. He had just given her proof that his motives for wanting to marry her were not love. Why hadn't she seen it right from the beginning? Why had Jared seen it when she hadn't?

Hilda's eyes were on her often as the day progressed, but it was not until it was time for Alice to go home that the woman spoke to her. 'Are you a friend of Tony's?' Her voice was pleasant, even though there was an assessing hardness in her eyes.

'We've met,' agreed Alice.

'But there's nothing between you?'

'Heavens, no!' she said vehemently, and that was the truth. There never had been and now there never would be.

'I see,' answered Hilda. 'Thank you. I like Tony we've had some good times together. I like to think it's more than just a holiday romance. He tells me he's going to settle down here.'

'I wouldn't know about that,' said Alice. 'I really don't know him very well at all.' This was becoming more and more clear with every day that passed. In England she had thought she knew him so well. How he had changed!

A few minutes after one she walked out of the salon and bumped into Jared. Tony was nowhere in sight. He took one look at her face and asked what was wrong.

'Nothing,' she shrugged.

'You didn't get on with Hilda?'

'Hilda's all right.'

'But something's happened, I can tell.'

'Stop it, Jared—nothing's wrong!' she hissed, her eyes flashing angrily.

It was his turn to shrug. 'Come on, I'll take you home. I had planned on lunch out somewhere, but I don't think you're in the mood.'

Nor was Alice in the mood to go back to Blue Vista. 'I'd prefer to eat out,' she said quietly.

His brows rose. 'If you're sure?'

She nodded.

He led the way to his car and they left the town behind and he drove to a tiny village a couple of miles away. He stopped at a place where tables were set out beneath an awning of palm-leaves. It looked nothing, and yet the food was superb, and Alice discovered she had quite an appetite.

'Feeling better?' asked Jared when she had forked up her last mouthful.

'Mm, yes,' she nodded, 'much better.' She felt relaxed now, and happier, and she knew it was Jared's presence.

'Perhaps now you can tell me what upset you?'

She swallowed hard. 'It was Tony,' she admitted.

Jared frowned. 'He came into the salon?'

Alice nodded

'To see you?'

'Not to see me,' she explained. 'Hilda. I think he was making a date with her, and it looked as though it wasn't the first time.'

'I see.' He watched her face closely. 'And it hurt, his dating another woman?'

'What do you think?' It was still important to her to carry on the charade.

'That you're a fool. Can't you see now what he's like?'

Alice shrugged. 'I suppose so.'

'I imagine he's lining someone else up in case you back out,' said Jared gruffly. 'Hilda's not short of money. Whitesands isn't her only salon.'

'I don't think I can carry on working for her,' said Alice.

'That's all right,' he said. 'It was a temporary job anyway.'

She frowned. 'You didn't tell me that,' and then, as she saw Jared's smug expression, 'You knew! You knew about him and Hilda? You did it deliberately.'

'Ten out of ten,' he said. 'And it worked, didn't it?

Sooner than I expected.'

She glared at him furiously. 'You're a devious swine!'

'Plain talking didn't work,' Jared shrugged.

'I hate you! What am I going to do now? Are there any more jobs going anywhere?'

'Actually,' he smiled, 'I think you might not want to go to work when you hear my news. The school holidays are starting, and Luke's coming home tomorrow.'

# CHAPTER SEVEN

ALICE could not believe that Jared thought she would be pleased to see his son—a child her grandfather had idolised, who had taken her own place in Daniel Alexander's heart. How wrong he was! 'I'm sorry I can't share your enthusiasm,' she said brusquely. 'I'm not interested in Luke, not one little bit.'

His face hardened. 'Alice, how can you spite a five-year-old? Whatever happened in the past has nothing at all to do with him. He's a sweet lovable little boy and——'

'Which doesn't mean I have to love him too,' she cried. 'I don't want to see Luke, I'll move out, I'll——'

'You'll do nothing of the sort,' he cut in coldly. 'As a matter of fact it will help Luke having you here. He misses Mary. Mrs Bell isn't the same.'

'She doesn't love him either, huh?'

He closed his eyes and clenched his fists, and Alice wondered why he was getting so worked up. He couldn't order her to love the child, could he? She liked children normally, but this one was different. He belonged to another life, a life in which she had no part.

'Let's go,' he said abruptly, and it appeared she had no further say in the matter.

They returned to the villa and Alice did not see him again that afternoon, although his car still stood outside. She took a dip in the pool and rested on her bed, and eventually joined him for dinner.

But he did not seem inclined to talk and Alice did not eat much, excusing herself as soon as she could and going

117

back up to her room.

The next morning he had left the house when she got up, and Alice guessed he had gone to fetch his son. She toyed with the idea of moving out, but there was not much sense in it. Now that she had learned the truth about Tony she could not stay with him, and she would be even lonelier than she was now.

It was almost lunch time when they arrived. The car pulled up and she watched them from the library window. Jared got out first and walked around to the other side of the car. Alice expected to see Luke scrambling out, full of excitement like all boys of his age, but instead Jared lifted him into his arms.

She frowned, wondering if he were ill, but the boy was laughing and talking, and soon they were out of sight. She moved away from the window but stayed in the room, one half of her wanting to go and meet them, the other holding reluctantly back. It was several minutes before she heard the little boy's voice. 'Where is she? Where's Alice? I want to see her!'

Slowly she emerged from the room and looked at the two of them. Jared stood tall and proud, smiling down at his son. And from his crutches Luke looked curiously up at her.

Alice swallowed, trying hard to hide her sudden shock. Poor kid! What had happened? 'Hello, Luke.' She smiled, her animosity forgotten. He was like a miniature version of Jared, the same sunny fair hair, the same dark blue eyes, the square jaw.

He balanced on one crutch and held out his hand. 'Hello, Alice. I hope you're going to play with me? She's pretty, Daddy. You didn't tell me she was pretty.'

Jarred touched his son's shoulder. 'Didn't I? I must have forgotten.'

Alice shook his hand solemnly. How grown-up he

sounded! 'Thank you for saying I'm pretty. You're not so bad yourself. What have you been doing?' Actually there looked nothing wrong with him. He wore brown shorts and sandals, and a yellow T-shirt, and he looked tanned and healthy and just like any other five-year-old boy.

'Didn't you know I can't walk? But it doesn't matter,' grinned Luke. 'These are my legs. I can do what I like on them.' And he proceeded to race on his crutches at tremendous speed around the hall. 'I can even play football,' he added proudly. 'Like this.' And he balanced on his crutches and swung the lower half of his body forward, his feet aiming at an imaginary ball.

Alice watched in admiration and pity, then turned to Jared, her eyes pained. 'Why didn't you tell me?' she asked.

'Were you interested?' he clipped.

She looked away guiltily.

'If I'd told you Luke was a cripple you'd have thought I was after sympathy. Isn't that so?' His eyes were hard on her face.

'I'm sorry,' Alice whispered, feeling thoroughly ashamed.

'Don't be,' he said roughly. 'Luke's conquered his handicap. He's a boy in a million.' All his fatherly pride showed on his face as he looked down at his son.

'You promised we could go swimming, Daddy.'

'So I did. There's just time before lunch. Come on, let's see how good you are.'

'I'm good. I'm very good,' Luke claimed importantly. 'Miss Gaymer says so. Are you coming, Alice?'

She looked hesitantly at Jared, who nodded.

'I'll go and put my swimming costume on.'

'Me and Daddy don't bother,' Luke told her.

Alice felt her cheeks redden.

Jared laughed. 'But today Daddy's wearing trunks,' he said. 'We can't embarrass Alice, can we?'

'But I don't want to. I——'

'You don't have to,' said Jared gently. 'Alice isn't interested in little boys like you.'

'Who is she interested in? You Daddy?'

Jared looked at Alice, his lips curling in amusement. 'I don't know, Luke. Perhaps you'd better ask her?'

But Alice did not wait for the question. 'I'll see you two later,' she said, and ran up to her room. The thought of Jared swimming in the nude had sent all sorts of unwanted thoughts racing through her mind.

In the end she decided not to join them. She had never swum with Jared before and suddenly she found the thought too daunting.

But when they sat down to lunch she was bombarded with questions from Luke. 'Why didn't you come? he wanted to know

'I thought you might like your daddy to yourself,' Alice explained.

'I was waiting for you.'

'I'm sorry,' she said.

'Can't you swim?' he asked next. 'Don't you like swimming?'

'I love it,' she smiled, 'and I promise that tomorrow I'll join you.' With a bit of luck Jared would be back at work, unless he was having time off to be with his son?

Immediately after lunch Luke disappeared, but when Alice would have left the room too Jared detained her. His voice was cold. 'Alice, why did you snub Luke?'

She frowned. 'Did I?'

'You know damn well you did!' he snarled. 'You made a promise and then never turned up.'

'I explained why,' she said defensively.

'He kept asking where you were,' he insisted. 'I thought when you saw Luke you might change your mind and show some interest. Have you any idea what that kid's been through?'

Alice swallowed a painful lump in her throat. 'I can imagine. Will he ever get better?'

Jared shook his head. 'He was born like it. It's pretty complicated, but something to do with a deformity in his hips and lower spine. My God, you'd think with today's technology they'd be able to do something, but no. The kid's had operations to straighten his back, but he'll never be able to walk.'

Alice looked down at the floor. What a tragedy! And what could she say? 'Your wife—she——'

'My wife freaked out when her son was born deformed.' There was so much anger and hurt in Jared's face that Alice wished she had not asked. 'She wanted nothing to do with him.'

'Oh, Jared, I'm sorry!'

'Don't be,' he snarled. 'Roxana was a mistake. It wasn't a happy marriage, though lord knows I tried. I discovered a selfish side to her that she'd previously kept hidden. She didn't even want children. It took me years to persuade her that our life would be more complete. And then what happened?' He smashed his fist into his palm. 'She blamed me, of course.'

'Most women change their minds once their baby is born,' Alice remarked.

'Not Roxana. And especially when she discovered Luke wasn't perfect. She gave me an ultimatum, either the baby or her.'

'And you chose Luke?'

'I had to. I love that child. I still fail to understand how she could disown him completely.'

'Daniel did it to my mother,' she said quietly.

'That was different,' he growled. 'Your mother was quite capable of looking after herself. Luke was a helpless baby.'

So what happened?'

'I employed a full-time nurse to begin with. And Mary helped, of course. She was marvellous—I don't know what I would have done without her. In the end she took sole charge of him. It was a sad day when she died.'

'He seems a fiercely independent little boy,' said Alice. 'He does you proud.'

He nodded. 'He's gutsy. He's gone through a lot but always comes out smiling.'

'I'm sorry, Jared, that your marriage didn't work out.'

'I don't need pity,' he snarled. 'Nor does Luke. I just want you to accept him as he is. He needs a friend here. Mary was like a mother and a grandma and a friend all rolled into one. He misses her. And to be honest, it's too quiet here for a kid of his age. And obviously I can't spend as much time with him as I would like. Can I rely on you to help out?'

'Of course,' said Alice at once. She didn't need time to think about it. Luke had won her over straight away.

'You're sure?'

She nodded.

Jared took her hands and looked deep into her eyes. 'Thank you, Alice.'

She wanted him to kiss her, but he didn't. He merely squeezed her hands, then released her. 'Shall we go and see what he's up to?' he asked.

That night Tony phoned, but she told him she didn't want to see him again, and no matter how much he pleaded and persuaded he could not change her mind.

In the days that followed Luke introduced an air of gaiety to the place, and his laughter was infectious.

They swam frequently—he was like a fish in the water, his arms propelling him along with amazing power. Alice read to him and helped him to read some of his books.

They played Hide and Seek and Ludo, and Jared sometimes took them out.

If Jared was working she helped Luke get bathed and dressed and all the little jobs he could not manage. But when Jared was at home he looked after Luke himself, and Alice saw a side to Jared that she had not seen before—a caring, compassionate man with lots of love in his heart and so much patience and tenderness that she actually felt jealous of his son.

And then one day the phone rang, and it was Tony again. 'Alice, I must see you. Can we have dinner tonight?'

'I'm afraid that's impossible,' she said. 'Why don't you ask Hilda?'

He was silent for a moment. 'There was never anything serious between Hilda and me. She was a diversion, when you weren't around.'

'Really?' she challenged. 'I suppose the fact that Hilda's a wealthy woman doesn't mean a thing?'

'Alice!'

She snorted angrily. 'I'm beginning to see you as you really are, Tony. I wish I'd never let you come with me. I just want you to get out of my life.'

'Alice, no, you can't! I must see you—please! If not dinner, then now, for just a few minutes. Please!'

But she was firm in her refusal. 'No, Tony. Not now, not ever.'

'I'm coming over, you can't get rid of me that easily,' he threatened.

'Tony, I haven't time to talk to you. It's Luke's party today, and I'm very busy.'

'Luke? Who the hell is he?'

'Jared's son.'

'And you'd put him before me?'

'Yes, Tony.'

'This is ridiculous!' he complained.

'Is it? I don't think so. He's a smashing kid and I like him a lot, and I have no intention of spoiling his party just to chat to you.'

'Jared's using him to get you on his side,' sneered Tony. 'So that you won't feel too badly about the lad inheriting what should rightly have been yours.'

Alice sighed heavily. 'Luke has no idea my grandfather has left him anything. And now I've met the boy I can see exactly why my grandfather did it. Not that I'd expect you to understand, not in a thousand years. The best thing you can do, Tony, is go home. There's nothing for you here.' And with that she put down the phone.

'Bravo! Bravo!'

She wheeled round and saw Jared watching her.

'Eavesdropping again?' she asked crossly.

'All I heard was you giving Tony his marching orders,' he grinned.

She shrugged. 'It was what I had to do. He wanted to see me.'

'You could have gone.'

'And disappoint Luke?'

He smiled. 'I'm glad you like him. It means a lot to me.'

'Does it?' She gazed at him, her eyes wide.

'Yes, Alice.' Jared put his hand on her shoulders and lowered his head, then Luke came swinging into the room.

'Alice, Alice, come and look, come and look!'

And her attention was instantly taken up by the youngster. Mrs Bell had given him a jigsaw with giant pieces and he had finished it and wanted her to praise him.

'My, Luke, what a clever boy you are!' she smiled.

'I did it, all by myself. Look, that's a castle and that's a——'

Alice felt an arm across her shoulders and discovered that Jared had followed and was also looking down at the puzzle. She heard no more of Luke's excited chatter.

Jared's touch, though light, set her pulses racing, his nearness incited her, and she could not help wondering whether at last his feelings for her were changing.

He seemed so much closer these days. There was a subtle difference in their relationship. Would he be standing here like this if he did not feel something? Would he have wanted to kiss her? Had Luke brought them together?

Perhaps he had wanted to see how she and Luke reacted towards one another before disclosing his own feelings? Her adrenalin ran high and she turned her face up to him—and he kissed her.

Luke looked up at that precise moment and a delighted grin spread over his face. 'Are you going to marry my daddy?' he asked Alice.

Alice clapped hands to her hot cheeks and glanced anxiously at Jared. He did not look in the least perturbed.

'That's enough of that, my boy. But the answer is no. People have to be in love to get married.'

'And doesn't Alice love you?'

'Of course not,' said Alice quickly to hide her embarrassment. 'I'm only here because of my grandfather's will.'

'Will? What's a will?' asked Luke, frowning.

'A will is a kind of letter that people leave when they die,' Jared explained patiently. 'They write down what they want people to have.'

'Grandma died,' said Luke. 'And Gramps.'

'That's right,' commented his father. 'And Gramps asked Alice to come here, and if she's a good girl she'll get something that he's left her.'

Luke thought about that. 'I'm a good boy. What am I getting?'

Jared ruffled his hair. 'You'll get a good hiding if you carry on asking questions! How about putting this puzzle away? It will soon be time to get ready for your party.'

The boy's face lit up. 'Yes, yes! Alice will you help me?'

'No, she will not,' said Jared firmly. 'Alice is coming outside with me. I want to talk to her.'

About what? she wondered, following him into the garden.

'You mustn't mind Luke,' he said. 'He has a knack of asking awkward questions.'

'I didn't mind,' she said, but the colour flooded her cheeks once again. How she wished she did not blush! It had been a failing of hers all her life.

'And was it true, that you don't love me?'

Oh, Jared, she thought, what a question! Was he blind? Did he not know? What was he expecting her to say? How she wished she knew what his thoughts were. She couldn't say yes, it was far too humiliating. But if she said no it would be a lie. What could she say?

'I think you know how I feel about you,' she said.

Jared nodded slowly. 'I was your first love, but not your last, isn't that right? You still feel something for me, but it's purely physical. You have no intention of letting your heart rule your head a second time?'

'That's right,' she returned sharply. 'And I'm glad you know it. Is that all you wanted to discuss?'

'For the moment.' He looked at her long and hard, then swung away.

Alice felt disappointed. She had expected more. Instead he had accepted without question that she did not love him. She shrugged mentally and went indoors, asking Mrs Bell whether she could help her with the preparations for the party. But the housekeeper had everything under control, so she went up to her room and changed into a pair of slacks and a T-shirt, and soon afterwards the first of Luke's guests arrived.

It was a hilarious afternoon. Luke's disability in no way impaired his pleasure. Jared organised games and Luke often won, and not because anyone let him. He was so nimble on his crutches it was unbelievable. He had said they were his legs and they were, he could more or less do anything on them.

The children ate their way through mountains of food, and afterwards they went indoors and Jared played the piano and the children sang. Alice stood beside him and led them in their singing, and they were all disappointed when he stopped.

But as soon as Luke suggested Hide and Seek in the garden they all raced outside. Alice hid too, and was taken completely by surprise when Jared crept into the bushes beside her, his hand going over her mouth to stop her shouting out.

'You shouldn't be with me,' she protested laughingly, 'you should be somewhere on your own.'

'It's more fun like this.' He slid his arms around her and held her close.

Alice felt the blood surge along her nerve-streams. 'What will the children think if they find us?'

'Who cares?' he chuckled, tracing the outline of her mouth with a fingertip. 'You're a good singer, do you know that?'

'And you're a good pianist,' she returned, pleased by his compliment.

'Will you sing for me one of these nights?'

She flushed. 'I don't think so.'

'Are you shy?' he asked. 'There's no need to be. I thought we made a pretty good pair.'

'We entertained the children at least,' she said, making her tone deliberately light. 'Shh!' She pressed closer into the bushes. I think someone's coming.'

'There's only one way to stop me talking,' Jared said.

'And what's that? By——' But Alice got no further. His mouth claimed hers and all else was forgotten as her body filled with sensations.

She arched closer and held his head with her hands, feeling the springy wiriness of his hair, drinking in the exciting maleness of him, knowing the kiss could not last but enjoying it while she could.

When he put her from him Alice's eyes were shining, and he looked down at her with a smile. 'You look as though you enjoyed that as much as me.'

'Daddy—Alice! I've found you!'

Luke's excited voice broke into their private world and they whirled around. Luke was grinning. 'It's OK, you can carry on kissing,' he told them.

'Why, you cheeky young rascal!' But Jared was smiling all the same, and when his son disappeared he kissed Alice again. But it was a brief kiss this time. 'If we're not careful,' he chuckled, 'he'll bring the whole gang. I don't know about you, but I don't fancy being a peepshow.'

Soon it was time for the children to leave. Parents turned up and collected their respective offspring, while Alice wandered over to the pool and sat down on the grass, hunching her knees up to her chin. She always liked this spot when she wanted to be alone with her thoughts, and she had plenty to think about today.

But she had been there for no more than a few seconds when she heard Jared's raised voice. She frowned. Who was he talking to? Not Luke? He wouldn't shout at Luke like that.

She got up and hurried towards the house and to her dismay realised that the other person was Tony. She gave an inward groan. What did he want?

'No, I will not tell Alice you're here!' roared Jared. 'She doesn't want to see you—I happen to know she's made that perfectly clear. So get off my property now, otherwise I'll take great pleasure in throwing you off!'

Alice broke into a run. 'Jared, what's going on?' She rounded a corner of the house and practically bumped into them. They were facing each other like raging bulls, but the moment Tony clapped eyes on her a look of relief came over his face.

'Alice, thank goodness!' he exclaimed. 'Will you get this maniac off my back?'

'Alice, you keep out of this,' warned Jared, his eyes flaring.

'I want a word with Alice,' said Tony belligerently. 'You can't stop me doing that.'

'Oh yes, I can, and I will,' threatened Jared. 'You're not welcome here, Chatwin.'

'For Pete's sake, stop it!' yelled Alice, standing between the two of them. And then on a slightly quieter note, 'I think I ought to speak to Tony, Jared.'

His mouth tightened and he glared at her, then he transferred his gaze to Tony. 'OK, just five minutes, but no more.' And then to Alice, 'Call me if you need me.'

'She won't,' said Tony tightly.

Alice took Tony's arm and pulled him away. They were still eyeing each other hostilely, still spoiling for a fight. 'Come on, let's go and sit by the pool.'

'Who the hell does he think he is!' muttered Tony as they walked away. 'What right has he to keep me from seeing you?'

'It is his house,' said Alice soothingly.

'And you're my girlfriend.'

'Your friend,' corrected Alice.

'I'm still hoping to persuade you that you love me.'

They reached the pool and sat down on the canvas chairs. 'Jared overheard me telling you to go home,' Alice announced.

'Damn!' Tony swore loudly. 'But there's no reason why he shouldn't think it was a lovers' tiff. Is there?'

'Is that what you think it was?'

'I think he's trying to split us up,' said Tony.

'Why would he want to do that?'

'Because he wants to marry you himself.'

Her head jerked. 'Don't say we're back to that again. It's nonsense. He has no interest in me.'

'No?' he jeered. 'Then explain why I saw him kissing you not all that long ago.'

Alice frowned. 'Where were you?'

'I was around.'

'You were spying?'

'I was waiting for an opportunity to speak to you.'

'I didn't invite his kiss, if that's what you're saying!' she snapped.

'Neither did you resist him.'

Alice turned her head away impatiently. 'I really don't think what I do is any business of yours.'

He caught her chin and made her face him. 'I love you, Alice. We came here together. I thought I meant something to you. And I would have, if he hadn't got in the way.'

'You sound very sure of yourself,' she tossed scornfully.

'I am sure. Can you deny that you wouldn't have spent every minute of your time with me if Jared hadn't been here?'

'Of course not,' she said. 'But it still doesn't mean I would have fallen in love with you. You're just not my type. We've always been friends, Tony. You accompanied me—as a friend, nothing more. And I'd like to think that we can remain so. But as for anything else, you're deluding yourself. There's no spark of magic between us. There never will be.'

'And there is that "spark of magic" between you and Jared?' he demanded, his tone insulting.

'No!' she cried, feeling justified in denying her own emotions when they were not returned.

Tony eyed her quizzically for almost half a minute, then he hooked his hand round her nape and pulled her face towards him.

Alice suffered his touch, but when he kissed her she felt nothing, and when he would have deepened the kiss she struggled free.

'No, Tony!' she protested.

'Yes, Tony,' he insisted. 'I've kept my distance long enough. It's about time you realised how serious I am.'

'About what?' she scorned. 'Loving me, or my inheritance?'

'About you, of course,' he said thickly.

'Isn't it amazing,' she shot, 'how all of a sudden I've become an object of your sexual desires. This never happened in England. Is it the sun?'

'I've always loved you, Alice.'

'No, you haven't,' she tossed back. 'It wasn't until you heard about my grandfather's will that you began showing any real interest.'

'Alice, that's not true,' Tony protested. 'I thought I'd convinced you.'

'You prefer to ignore the way I feel because money means more to you than love. Perhaps you ought to find yourself a rich widow? Perhaps that's what you ought to be looking for. Perhaps——'

'Alice, damn you!' He caught her by the shoulders and hauled her to her feet, then taking her face between his hands he claimed her lips with his. He was like a man possessed, as if by kissing her he could make her love him.

She pushed against him, she rained furious blows on his shoulders and back, all to no avail. She felt revolted by his touch and could not believe that this was the same

Tony who had helped her through the black days after her mother's death. This was a side of him she had never seen, and one she did not like. He frightened her.

'That's enough!'

She suddenly heard Jared's voice above Tony's laboured breathing.

'Let her go.'

Tony stilled, for just a second, before renewing his assault on her mouth, his tongue forcing its way between her lips. She felt nauseous and strained with all her might to push him from her.

Quite how it happened she did not know, but suddenly Jared was standing between them. His face was pale and taut and grim, and his hand was on Tony's shoulder. 'Don't ever touch Alice again, Chatwin, do you hear? Another time you might not get off so lightly!'

Tony glared but said nothing.

'Now get off my property,' Jared grated through his teeth, 'and don't ever return. You're not welcome. You never were and you never will be.'

'Alice?' pleaded Tony, but she looked at him with complete revulsion, shuddering and turning away.

Tony flushed an ugly red and wrenched himself free from Jared's grasp. 'OK, you win,' he sneered, 'for now. But I'll get my own back, you see if I don't!'

He slouched away, and Alice could not look at him. Her whole body was tense, and when Jared gently touched her she flinched, her eyes wide and filled with horror and a darker blue than normal.

'It's all right,' he said softly. 'He's gone now.' And then, on an angry note, 'I should never have let him see you. It was all my fault.

'No,' she insisted. 'You couldn't have known—I didn't know myself. He's never acted like that before.

Oh, God, it was awful! I feel so sick.'

'Come into the house,' Jared suggested quietly. Alice nodded and began to walk slowly towards the building, resisting Jared's offer of an arm, though goodness knew her legs felt weak enough.

'Why did he do it?' she asked huskily. 'Why did he force himself on me when he know I don't love him? I've never loved him. It must be the money he's after, as you said. I don't know what else it can be. But surely he doesn't think he can *make* me love him?'

'Don't think about him,' said Jared soothingly. 'He's sick. He's not worthy of even the most fleeting thought.' He took her into the lounge and poured her a brandy, then stood over her while she drank every drop.

The fiery liquid soon warmed and soothed her, her trembling ceased and she sat back and closed her eyes. But all she could see was Tony's face looming over hers, his lips hot and moist, his eyes full of crazed desire, and she shook her head, her face creased once again in anguish.

'Alice.' Jared sat down beside her and pulled her against him, and he was gentle and calm, stroking back her hair from her forehead, murmuring words of comfort, that gradually she relaxed and nestled up to him quite voluntarily.

'Better now?' he asked after a few minutes.

She nodded. 'I'm sorry.'

'Hell, don't apologise. It wasn't your fault.'

'I should have been able to handle him,' Alice muttered.

'When a man's mind is made up there's not much you can do about it, unless you see it coming.'

'I never expected Tony to behave like that,' she explained.

'What brought it on, do you know?'

She nodded. 'He saw us kissing.'

'I see,' he said. 'So it was jealousy?'

'As well as anger, because I told him if it was only money he was interested in to go and find himself a rich widow.'

Jared laughed. 'I like that. So you finally came to your senses.'

Alice nodded self-consciously.

'You're well rid of him. I imagine he'll go back to England now he knows there's no hope. Unless of course he takes your advice,' he grinned.

She smiled. 'I don't imagine there are many rich widows in these parts. None who'd be interested in Tony anyway. He's a creep!'

Luke chose that moment to come into the room. 'Who was that man, Daddy?'

Jared smiled fondly at his son. 'Just somebody.'

Alice wondered how much he had seen. He must have been looking out of one of the windows.

'Why were you shouting?' Luke wanted to know.

'He wasn't supposed to be here,' replied Jared softly.

Luke nodded. 'He didn't look very happy when he went away. Why did he come?'

'You ask too many questions. Come and sit here with us and tell me how you enjoyed your party.'

For ten minutes Luke chattered, then he suddenly remembered something he wanted to do. Jared handed him his crutches and the little boy left the room quite happily.

'To go back to our earlier conversation,' said Jared, 'I should be interested to hear exactly why you wanted me to believe that you loved Tony. Were you perhaps trying to hide your real feelings? Do you still imagine yourself in love with me?'

# CHAPTER EIGHT

ALICE opened her eyes wide. 'Jared Duvall, how could you even think such a thing?'

'Quite easily,' he grinned.

'Well, I can assure you it's not true,' she said firmly. He was never going to get her to admit to loving him, not when he showed no signs of returning such a feeling. 'So don't flatter yourself that my pretending to love Tony had anything to do with you.'

'It was Tony you were fooling?'

She grimaced. 'No, it wasn't. He knew all along how I felt about him, but he wanted me to keep up the charade, because—well, because—he doesn't like you.'

'Likewise,' interrupted Jared.

'And he thought you might want to marry me.' Lord, this was embarrassing! Alice wished she had never started. 'He thought you might be after Grandfather's money as well.'

A look of astonishment spread over Jared's face. 'Why would I want Daniel's money? I have enough of my own.'

'I tried to tell him that.'

'But he still thought I was after you?'

She nodded unhappily.

'And what would have been your reaction had I asked you to marry me?' asked Jared.

Alice swallowed hard and avoided his eyes. 'I wouldn't have believed you meant it.'

'Why?' he frowned.

'Because—I know you don't love me. You never have.

135

You were trying to find out all you could about me so that you could report back to Daniel. I stupidly read more into it than there was.'

'And now you're over me?'

She felt her heart pumping furiously.

'Alice, look at me!'

With an effort she dragged her gaze back to his. How dry her mouth was!

'I'm waiting.'

'I'm over you,' she whispered.

Jared's eyes narrowed. 'You don't sound very sure.'

'I am.' She jutted her chin now and made her voice strong. 'It would be pretty stupid of me if I wasn't, wouldn't it?'

'Why do you say that? What's stupid about loving someone?'

'It's stupid if that person doesn't return your love. It's wasting your life.'

'And Alice doesn't want to waste her life?' he mocked.

She shook her head angrily. 'I don't know why we're having this conversation.' Unless it was his way of taking her mind off Tony and what he had done to her. Could it be that? If so it was working. Her thoughts were of Jared now and no one else.

'I find it very interesting,' he said.

'Well, I find it boring,' she lied. 'I think I'd like to go to my room.'

Jared stood immediately and held out his hand to help her up, but she ignored it and walked away without looking at him again, though she felt his gaze boring into her back, and she would have liked more than anything to turn to him and have him kiss her like he had earlier.

Once in her room, she lay down on the bed. Her body pulsed with her need of Jared, and she decided she was a fool to deny herself this pleasure. He would be only too willing to comply were she to give him any encouragement, of that she felt sure.

She closed her eyes and let her thoughts waft, then she heard Luke's shrieks of laughter as Jared got him ready for bed. She knew it was time to shower now and dress for dinner, and she reluctantly pushed herself up.

When she was ready she popped in to see Luke to make sure he was all right. He was fast asleep, his face angelic. He had had a busy day. Alice bent low and kissed him, then heard a sound—and there was Jared. She had not realised he was still in the room.

She did not mind that he saw her kissing his son. She made no secret of the fact that she loved the child. With a pleased smile he took her hand and they walked down the stairs together.

There seemed to be a subtle change in their relationship. Whether it was because Tony was now well and truly banished from the scene, or whether it was because her own feelings were gradually changing, Alice did not know, but whatever, she felt more at peace with Jared than she had since her arrival.

After dinner they took their coffee through into the lounge and sat talking easily for over an hour. Then Jared excused himself to check on Luke, and Alice got up and stretched her arms and took a walk around the room.

At the collection of photographs she stopped and picked up the one of herself and her mother, feeling suddenly sad. If her grandfather hadn't been such a stubborn old fool they might have lived here, might have spent all their lives in this beautiful place. Instead her mother had died without ever experiencing the luxury he could have given her. Her whole life had been one long, uphill struggle—and all because of one man.

Alice put down the photograph and picked up the one of Daniel. Her lips were grim as she studied it. There were certain resemblances between Daniel and her mother. They both had the same stubborn chin, the same strong-boned face, the same determined look about the eyes. It had been a battle of the strongest, but it had ended in stalemate. They had both suffered because of their own obstinacy, and it had got them nowhere.

'I miss him,' said Jared's voice over her shoulder.

She whirled to find him studying the picture with her. 'I hope you don't expect me to sympathise?' she shot coldly.

He frowned. 'It would obviously be foolish of me to think you might.'

'I really fail to understand how he could have distanced himself from his daughter for so long, or even how he did it in the first place. The man had no heart. Could you do it to Luke?'

He shook his head.

'Say for instance he was seventeen or eighteen and he committed a crime—maybe even murder. Would you stand by him, or disown him?'

'I'd stand by him,' he said quietly.

'And so would any caring parent,' snapped Alice. 'I sometimes wish, especially now I've come here and feel I know him better, that we had met. I'd have loved to tell him exactly what I think of him.'

'He'd have won you over,' Jared said confidently. 'Daniel deeply regretted what he did. If he could have turned back the clock he would have done.'

Alice eyed him scornfully. 'What stopped him coming to see my mother? I'm sure all she was waiting for was some move on his part. I know in the early years, especially just after I was born, she tried to see him, but he didn't want to know. He proved that by leaving England. The message came across loud and clear.'

'He was hurt, bitter, disappointed, disillusioned. All those things. He felt she'd let him down.

'And didn't he let her down?' she flashed. Her face was animated now, her eyes a brilliant blue, her cheeks flushed. This was a subject she felt very strongly about. 'Doesn't a girl need her family behind her at times like those? Didn't he think she ever regretted what she had done? Didn't he realise she needed his love and support?'

'At the time he didn't think that way,' admitted Jared. 'But as time passed he frequently grew depressed. He questioned himself as to whether he was to blame. Don't forget he'd been both mother and father to her for several years. He began to feel he was the one at fault, that he hadn't instilled the right moral values into her, that if he'd been a good father she would never have gone out and got herself pregnant.'

'Got herself pregnant?' questioned Alice, her lip curling with distaste. 'You make it sound as though she had sex for the sake of sex! For goodness' sake, she loved the boy! He was the one who had the low moral values. He didn't care two hoots about her.'

'And she hadn't the good sense to see that?'

'He led her on.'

Jared sniffed disbelievingly. 'Surely a girl can tell if a man's in love with her or if he only wants to get her between the sheets?'

'Not if she's besotted with him, which my mother was. He hurt her deeply. She never loved another man.'

'You can't blame Daniel for that,' Jared said coolly.

'No, it was over between them in any case, even before she discovered she was pregnant. So first my mother had the upset of losing him, then the discovery that she was having his baby, and then the trauma of being disowned by her father. And when you're only seventeen it's a lot to take.'

Jared nodded. 'I appreciate that.'

'And yet you still stick up for Daniel. All I can say is, he must have changed one hell of a lot—unless he never showed you that particular side of his nature?'

'I think I can say I knew Daniel fairly well, and I think there's something you ought to see, something that might change your mind about things.'

Alice frowned. 'Like what?'

He pulled open a drawer in the table which held the collection of photographs and reaching out a packet of letters he handed them to her.

She looked at him enquiringly.

'Read them,' he said.

'Who are they from?'

'Your mother.'

Alice gasped. 'What? My mother never wrote to him.'

'Daniel wrote to her too.'

'*No!*' She shook her head wildly. 'I don't believe that.'

'I'm afraid you'll have to. Read them, Alice.'

There were three letters in all. The first had been written twelve years ago, when Alice was only ten. It was in response to a letter from Daniel. Whatever he had asked, Gillian's reply was short and cruel.

> You disowned me competely, Father. I'm no longer your daughter, and Alice is not your granddaughter. I don't want to see you or hear from you again.

Alice swallowed a sudden lump in her throat and opened the second letter. This was dated a few months before Jared's visit to England.

> I told you once before, Father, that I want nothing to do with you. You left it too late.

That was all. Alice looked at Jared, who was watching her intently. Her face had paled now and her hands were trembling as she slowly shook her head in disbelief. She could not believe that her mother had written these words. Her mother had always denied that Daniel had ever tried to get in touch with her.

The third and final letter was dated twelve months ago, and it was even more cruel and taunting.

Why are you telling me you're not well? Do you expect sympathy? I got none when I needed it and you deserve none now. You let me down when I needed you. It took you ten years to make the first move—ten long years. Have you any idea what that did to me! If you'd tried just once, in the first year, or the second or even the third, I would have responded. I needed your love and support. But not now, not any longer. I've made my own life and I don't need you. Don't write to me again, because I shan't answer.

By the time she had finished reading Alice was close to tears. She found it difficult to believe that her mother had written these letters, that she could remain so hostile when her father was dying. Had he killed absolutely every ounce of compassion in her? And why had her mother never mentioned that he had written? *Why?*

'So you see,' Jared said quietly, 'Daniel did have a change of heart. He wasn't entirely the hard man you thought him.'

Alice jutted her chin. 'Ten years,' she derided. 'It took him ten years.

'That was unfortunate,' he admitted, 'but it needn't have been too late. Gillian proved to be more unforgiving than him.'

'Because she was the one who'd been hurt most!'

'You think your mother was right to reject his pleas for a reunion?'

Alice looked down at her hands. 'Not entirely.' And

then on a firmer note, 'But I can understand.'

'I can't,' he said. 'No one should bear a grudge for that long. Nor could Daniel believe she could be so hard. That's why he sent me over, to see what type of a woman she'd turned into.'

'And what did you find?' Alice demanded.

'On the surface a loving and caring person—a gentle woman, even. But inside she was hard and bitter. I tried my hardest to persuade her to see Daniel, but she wounds were too deep, the scars had never healed.'

'And even so Daniel wrote yet again?'

'One last attempt because he knew he hadn't many more months to live. He cried when he received Gillian's letter. He broke down altogether. He said he might write to you instead, but I told him that your mother had done a good job on you too and that he would get no joy. In his last months he retreated into himself, he sat for hours thinking, looking at his photographs, wishing, hoping. Dying.'

'Don't!' cried Alice. 'It wasn't my fault.'

'Wasn't it?' Jared eyes grew hard. 'Did you have to follow in your mother's footsteps? Weren't you curious? Didn't you ever want to see your grandfather? Didn't you miss him? You had no father, you could have had a grandfather.'

'I didn't want one who didn't care about me when I was born, when I was little, when I needed him most. I did without then, I could do without afterwards.' And on a defiant note she added, 'I never missed him. As far as I was concerned he never existed.'

His eyes narrowed angrily. 'So why did you bother to write and tell him Gillian had died?'

Alice shrugged carelessly. 'Actually my mother always said I was never to let him know if anything did happen to her.'

'So why did you?'

She pulled a face, announcing casually, 'It seemed the right thing to do.'

'It was,' Jared said roughly. 'You've no idea how it pleased Dan. Not Gillian dying, of course, he was cut up about that, but you getting in touch. He thought there was light at the end of the tunnel after all. It was a pity he died a couple of days later. But at least you gave him some happiness.'

He took her hands suddenly. 'I'm sorry, Alice, to put you throught this. But I think you had a right to know.'

'Sorry? *Sorry?*' she cried, snatching away from him. 'I don't think so. 'I think you took a perverse delight in showing me those letters, in watching my face as I read them, seeing my hurt. What were you hoping to achieve? Do you think I'll now see my mother as the baddie and Daniel as the goodie?'

'No.' He shook his head. 'Knowing you as I do, Alice, I'd never think that. You're as stubborn as your mother, as stubborn as Dan. You're all three of the same mould.'

'That's right!' she sparred.'What I want to know is why you didn't show me those letters earlier?'

'I didn't think you were in the right frame of mind to read them.'

'And what made you think now was the right time?' she asked aggressively.

He shrugged. 'For one of the few times since you've been here we weren't arguing, you were relaxed in my company, we were almost friends.'

'Not any more,' Alice said hardly. 'I'm going up to my room, Jared. I have a lot of thinking to do.'

'About what?' he frowned.

'My mother's letters.'

'You can't alter facts.'

'I wish she'd told me,' Alice sighed.

'Would it have made any difference? Would you have written to Dan, or would you have taken her side and agreed with what she said?'

Alice chewed her bottom lip. 'Actually, I think she went a bit over the top. She could have found a more polite way of telling him she wasn't interested. Or she needn't have written at all. It might have been kinder.'

'It would,' he said.

Alice nodded. 'Goodnight, Jared.'

'Goodnight, Alice.' His mouth was grim.

When she looked back from the doorway he was returning the letters to the drawer, then he picked up the photograph of Daniel and held it in his hands, studying it intently.

He really had loved that man, thought Alice, and deep down inside her she wished, for the first time, that she had known him too.

She slowly climbed the stairs. She had at long last learned that there was another side to Daniel than the one she had heard about from her mother. He had deeply regretted cutting his daughter out of his life, but he had left it too late to make amends.

In her room she closed the door and dragged off her clothes, sliding between the sheets and staring wide-eyed at the ceiling. How awful to die with the knowledge that your own daughter hated you, that she had never, ever, in over twenty years, found it in her heart to forgive.

For all that time Daniel had had to live under a cloud of despair. He had found happiness with Mary, but in the end he had died a lonely, broken man.

It was a long time before Alice fell asleep, and when she awoke the next morning she wondered why she felt so unhappy. Then memories returned, and with them an even deeper anger towards Jared.

He should have told them both when he came to England who he was, why he was there. Maybe then he would have been able to persuade her mother to see Daniel. The rift might have been healed. And why was she thinking like this? Surely she wasn't growing soft? Daniel deserved all he'd got, didn't he?

She got up and showered and went down to breakfast. Luke was sitting at the table, but Jared had gone to work.

'Why does he have to go?' complained Luke. 'Why can't he stay at home with me?'

'Because he has to earn some money. This house costs a lot to run, and there's your school fees and——'

'I don't have to go to school,' insisted Luke.

'You'd be pretty bored here if you didn't,' Alice pointed out.

'I'm glad you're here,' he said with a quick smile. 'I like you, Alice.'

'And I like you. Did you enjoy your party?'

He nodded enthusiastically.

'What do you want to do today?'

'Can we go to the beach?'

She shook her head. 'Not without Daddy. He gave me strict instructions.'

Luke pulled a face but accepted it. 'Will you help me build a spaceship with my Lego?'

Alice nodded.

'And afterwards we'll play in the pool with my new ball, it's huge, have you seen it?'

'I have,' she confirmed.

'I'd like to go in the pool first, but Daddy says I mustn't swim when I've just eaten. Why?'

'Because you might get tummyache.'

'Oh,' he said. 'I wouldn't like that.'

He was easily pleased, and not at all spoilt or pampered as one might except with a boy like him, and Alice realised even more than ever how much she had missed having a father. Her mother had done her best, but it was not the same.

By the same token, Luke needed a mother. Jared should marry again and provide him with one before he was much older. But it was surprising how much this thought hurt.

After breakfast they built their spaceship and played in the pool, then they had a light lunch and Luke went up to his room to rest. Alice walked in the garden—and got the shock of her life when Tony jumped out from behind the bushes, gripping her arm fiercely and forcing her towards his car.

'Tony, what are you doing? Let me go. *Let me go!*'

But his grip never slackened, and once she was in his car he drove away from the house at tremendous speed. Alice feared for her safety. The road was narrow and winding and not meant for rally driving like this.

'Where are we going?' she demanded, her voice coming out in a squeak. 'Where are you taking me?'

'We have to talk,' said Tony. 'Where we can't be disturbed. I've had enough of Duvall pushing his nose in.'

'I don't think we have anything to talk about,' said Alice. 'We said it all yesterday.'

'You said what you wanted to say, I didn't get much chance.'

He veered crazily along the road, almost out of control. Alice shut her eyes and clung to the edge of her seat. She risked a glance at him a few seconds later and he was grinning maniacally, enjoying it, deriving a thrill from the speed and near misses.

She could smell whisky on his breath and groaned inwardly. She would be lucky if she got out of this alive. But somehow, miraculously, they reached the bottom of the mountain in one piece, and Tony drove until they found a secluded spot, then he cut the engine and turned to face her.

'What do I have to do, Alice, to convince you that I love you?'

'Nothing,' she said.

His eyes narrowed. 'You mean you believe me?'

'Do I look that stupid?' she demanded. 'I shall never believe you. *Never.*'

His face contorted angrily. 'You were enjoying my kiss until that rat Duvall intervened.'

'Like hell I was! You make me sick, Tony, do you know that? You revolt me. I wish I'd never brought you here with me!'

He grinned. 'But you did, and you're not going to get rid of me. It's true, Alice, I am after your money—I might as well admit it. A nice little inheritance that will set me up for the rest of my life. I shall really enjoy living here. You as my wife, Blue Vista as my home. We'll soon turn Duvall out. We'll take him to court, make them see how he fiddled your grandfather.'

Alice was appalled. 'Tony, you're crazy! I have no intention of marrying you, and you can't make me.'

'No, I don't suppose I can,' he admitted surprisingly. 'In which case I'll settle for a share of the money. And if you don't agree, do you know what I'm going to do?'

He paused while she looked at him with approaching horror.

'I'm going to make sure that something happens to Jared's son.'

Alice gasped. 'You can't! You'd never get away with it. Besides, that's blackmail.'

'So,' Tony shrugged, 'what's the kid to me? Nothing, except that he stands to inherit some of your money.' His lip curled in a sneer. 'No one should have it except you. Blue Vista should be yours. It's all yours. And I want a share in it.'

'You're mad!' she cried. 'You're out of your mind! Take me back this instant!'

'Not until you agree.'

She tilted her chin. 'Never!'

'You don't care what happens to Luke?'

'You wouldn't dare harm him.'

'No? You wait and see.'

'I don't believe you, Tony. You're bluffing. I believe you want the money, but I don't think you'd ever harm Luke. It's too risky, you'd get caught. I for one would know it was you who'd done it.'

'Don't worry, I'd make sure no one ever suspected me. It would be an entirely natural accident, no false play at all. I've worked it all out, Alice. There's only you who can stop it.'

Alice could hardly breathe. She did not want to believe him, but he sounded so sure of himself. She shook her head. 'Tony, what's got into you? You're insane! Is money really all that important?'

'To me it is.'

'But I might not inherit much.'

'You will,' he said confidently.

'I want you to take me back,' she said.

'What is it then, you split fifty-fifty with me, or Duvall's son gets——'

'I need time to think,' said Alice.

Tony frowned. 'It should be a simple decision.'

'Well, it isn't!' she spat.

'You're going to tell Duvall?' he snarled suspiciously.

'No,' she said faintly. 'I promise you that.'

'You'd better not, or I might make things nasty for you as well.'

Alice closed her eyes and leaned back in her seat. She could not believe that this was the same Tony. To her relief he started the car and drove back up the mountain. He dropped her outside the gates, then left.

'Don't forget,' were his parting words. 'Not one word to Duvall.'

As she walked into the house the first person she saw was Jared. He appeared to be waiting for her, and he was furiously angry. 'Where the hell have you been?' he demanded.

Alice groaned inwardly. As if she hadn't had enough with Tony, without him starting now! 'Out,' she said tightly.

'With Tony Chatwin?'

Her eyes widened. How did he know? 'So what if I have?'

'My God,' he rasped, 'I hoped I was mistaken. I thought you'd come to your senses. What's going on?'

'What do you mean, what's going on? Tony's my friend. Why shouldn't I see him?'

'And only yesterday he tried to rape you!' he snarled harshly

He tried to kiss me,' she corrected.

'Against your will.'

'A girl can change her mind.' Alice wondered whether she ought to tell Jared what Tony had threatened. But what if Tony had simply been bluffing? He couldn't have meant it, surely? He wasn't like that. She needed to talk to Tony, to find out exactly what thoughts were going on his mind.

He had been drinking. Perhaps he did not know what he was saying? She felt sudden relief. That was it. It had been false bravado. She would go and see him again as soon as possible and everything would be all right. They would laugh about it and he would call himself a fool, and it would all be over.

'You need your head examining!' Jared went on.

'Chatwin's after your money, not you, I thought we agreed on that.'

'I have no intention of marrying him,' she protested. 'But that doesn't mean to say I can't see him now and then.'

'What did he want?' he asked bluntly.

'To apologise for yesterday,' she lied.

'That I don't believe,' he snarled. 'You're as pale as a ghost. The guy's upset you again.'

'You're upsetting me,' she riposted. 'You're the one who's spoiled things between me and Tony. Right from the start you had it in for him.'

'Because I saw him as you didn't. He's a hanger-on, and it's about time you realised it. I really thought after yesterday it was all over. Perhaps you wouldn't mind telling me what it is he has that draws you to him time and time again?'

Alice closed her eyes. 'I've had enough. I don't have to answer any of your questions.' And she stalked past him, climbing the stairs to her room, passing a wide-eyed Luke on the way.

She groaned inwardly. She had had no idea he was listening. Poor kid; he looked upset too. He stared at her and would have said something had not Jared called him to come down.

Her mind was in a tumult as she closed her bedroom door, and she stood against it, breathing shallowly and rapidly, wishing with all her heart that she had never come here in the first place.

# CHAPTER NINE

A FAINT tap on her bedroom door aroused Alice. She opened her eyes and sat up. She had not really been asleep, simply trying to relax, though it was not easy when her mind was so full.

The tap came again, still faint. It could not be Jared—he wouldn't have knocked so lightly, nor indeed would he have waited for her to answer. He would have barged in and said what was on his mind.

She walked across and opened the door, and there stood Luke, his face blotchy and tear-stained, and looking as though he was ready to burst into tears all over again.

'Luke!' Alice stooped down so that her face was on a level with his. 'What's wrong?' When he did not answer, she backed into the room. 'Come on in. Come and sit down.'

He did so, his head bent, and lowered himself into a chair. She took his crutches and leaned them against the wall, then sat on the edge of the bed facing him.

'It's my fault,' he whimpered.

Alice frowned. 'What's your fault?'

'Daddy shouted at you.' Luke's lips trembled and he valiantly fought back his tears.

'But how could that be because of you?' she asked softly, taking his hands and holding them between her own.

'Because—because I told him you'd gone out with that man.'

'With Tony?' frowned Alice. 'How could you have

known?'

'I saw you.' He looked down at their hands. 'I was looking through my bedroom window and I saw you get in his car. He was the same man who was here yesterday, wasn't he?'

She nodded.

'I didn't know Daddy would be cross, really I didn't. He asked me where you was and I told him, and then he shouted at you when you came back. I don't think he likes you seeing that man.' His tears began to flow freely now. 'It's all my fault. I'm sorry, Alice.'

Alice dropped to her knees and gathered him against her. 'It doesn't matter—really it doesn't. I'm not upset. Daddy shouted because I hadn't told anyone where I was going, not because it was Tony. You did the right thing telling him. He would have worried if he hadn't known where I'd gone.'

'Did I?' Luke looked at her anxiously through the blur of his tears.

'Of course you did,' she smiled, 'and you're not to worry about it any more. All right?'

He nodded, but he did not look too sure. 'Doesn't it make you want to cry, when Daddy shouts?'

'Yes, it does,' she admitted. 'You still feel like crying when you're grown up, but you pretend to be brave, and don't let anyone know that you're upset.'

'I wish I was grown up,' he sighed.

'Oh, Luke,' she murmured, holding him tight. 'You'll grow up soon enough.'

She reached a handkerchief and mopped his tears, and when he saw she wasn't cross or upset he soon cheered up. 'Will you come and help me do my jigsaw?' he asked.

'Of course I will,' Alice said softly, and they left the room together.

When it was time for Luke's tea, which he usually ate in

the kitchen with Mrs Bell, Alice wandered out into the garden and sat by the pool beneath the shade of the flamboyant tree. She closed her eyes and listened to the birds and the trickle of water coming down the mountainside.

It should have been peaceful, but it wasn't. She kept thinking about Tony's threats. She felt sure he wasn't serious, but on the other hand what if he was? What if he actually harmed Luke! She would never be able to forgive herself. Jared wouldn't forgive her either. The consquences didn't bear thinking about. She must tell Jared. Never mind about waiting to speak to Tony again; it might be too late.

Her mind made up, she relaxed in the warmth of the sun and fell asleep, and when she opened her eyes again Jared was sitting watching her. How long had he been here? Her stomach muscles twisted into knots at the thought of him silently studying her.

His face was quite serious and she had no idea what sort of a mood he was in. She smiled tentatively.'What time is it?' she asked.

'It will soon be time for dinner,' he said. 'Luke's already in bed. But before you get ready there's something I want to say to you.'

'I have something to say to you too, Jared.' It had to be said, and now. 'When I——'

He held up his hand. 'Hear me out first. Luke told me he'd apologised for telling tales on you.' His mouth quirked at the memory. 'I therefore think it only right that I should apologise too. You have a perfect right to choose your friends. It's wrong of me to interfere. How about calling a truce?'

The smile he gave her was enough to melt her bones, and it was a pity she had to wipe it off his face. 'I think,' she said slowly, 'when you hear what I have to say, you'll change your mind.'

Jared frowned, but he did not speak, waiting instead for her to go on.

'It's about Tony.'

His brows rose.

'He—he's——' Alice swallowed hard. How could she put Tony's threat into words? Perhaps it might be best if she started at the beginning. 'I didn't actually go with him of my own free will.'

Jared's eyes narrowed questioningly.

'He forced me. He came here and dragged me away.'

His chin lifted and there was a stillness about him that was frightening. 'Go on.'

'You were right all along. All he's after is the money he thinks I'll inherit.'

'So you've come to your senses?'

'No. *Yes!* You don't understand. He's blackmailing me ——'

'In what way?' crisped Jared.

'Well, first of all he said that—that if I wouldn't marry him then he'd settle for a half-share of the money he's sure I'll get. And if I don't agree to that then—he'll——' Alice bit her bottom lip anxiously, 'he'll—see that Luke has an—accident.'

Jared's head jerked. 'He's threatened my son?' He sounded as though he could not believe he had heard her correctly.

Alice grimaced, moving uncomfortably on her seat. 'I don't think he meant it. He was drunk.'

'It's enough that he's said it!' rasped Jared, his face pale, his eyes blazing, the skin tightly drawn across his chiselled bones.

'I wasn't going to tell you,' confessed Alice faintly. 'I was going to see him again. I'm sure it was the drink talking.'

'If he so much as touches one hair on my son's head I'll

kill him,' growled Jared, his clenched fists swinging at his side. 'I knew from the second I laid eyes on him that he wasn't to be trusted.'

'It's all my fault.' Alice felt like bursting into tears.

'You're damn right it's your fault!' he snapped. 'Why couldn't you have seen what type he was before bringing him here?'

She shook her head, her lips compressed. 'He changed,' she whispered.

'Leopards don't change their spots. You're too naïve, too gullible. He really must have thought he was on to a winner!' Jared closed his eyes and rocked on the balls of his feet.

'What are you going to do?' ventured Alice quietly.

He looked at her through narrowed eyes. 'Watch and wait. My first thoughts were to go and have it out with him, but no, I don't think that's the way to do it. I presume he made you promise not to tell me?'

She nodded. 'And I didn't actually say I wouldn't give him the money. I said I needed time to think.'

'Good, that will give me time to make my plans.' Jared paced up and down, deep in thought.

Alice stood up. 'I think I'll go and get changed for dinner,' she said softly, though the truth was she had never felt less like eating.'

She had walked only a few yards when he called her name. 'Alice, I'm not blaming you.'

Faint relief. 'But you're right,' she said. 'If I hadn't brought Tony with me, none of this would have happened.'

'Nothing is going to happen,' he said firmly. 'I'll make sure of that. I'll put Tony under close surveillance. And when you're alone with Luke you must make sure he's never out of your sight.'

She nodded. 'Of course.'

'And now I see no reason why we can't call that truce . . .'

'I'd like that,' she husked. 'Thank you, Jared, for not being too angry with me.'

'It's not your fault.'

She could not believe he was being so understanding, and there followed a few days of complete bliss. Alice neither saw nor heard from Tony, and Jared didn't mention him, though she felt sure he had already made whatever arrangements he deemed necessary.

He was a charming companion—funny, thoughtful, sexy. Alice had a wonderful time. He kissed her often, but she knew it meant nothing to him, and she refused to analyse her own feelings.

He had taken a few days off work and they went out on boat trips and car drives, they went fishing and snorkelling, and Luke always accompained them. He was never out of their sight for one second. He had a marvellous time too, and protested strongly when the day came for him to go back to school.

Once again he was close to tears. 'Will you be here when I come home next time?' he asked Alice as she poked her head through the car window to give him a last kiss.

Jared answered for her. 'Yes, she will.' And she was surprised by the firmness of his tone.

The house felt empty when they had gone, and Alice wandered around aimlessly. She had not heard from Tony again, and she came to the conclusion that his threats were empty ones, that it really had been the alcohol talking. Nevertheless, it was a relief that Luke had left the island. She had been under considerable strain. Now she could relax and enjoy herself with Jared.

But that was not so easy. Without Luke she felt

vulnerable. She loved Jared, she knew that without a shadow of doubt, but he did not return her feelings. He liked her, she thought, but he was only being nice to her for Daniel's sake. He wanted to make her three-month stay here enjoyable because he knew his old friend would expect it of him.

In the days that followed he flirted and teased, and there were times when Alice thought he was serious, when his kisses held more passion, when he held her as though he never wanted to let her go, but always he would break off and the next moment he would be talking about something else and she would wonder whether it was all wishful thinking on her part.

She decided that the best thing she could do was get a job, something to keep her mind occupied. And this time she would not ask Jared for help but find something for herself.

The morning after she had made this decision Alice phoned for a taxi as soon as Jared had left. She spent the whole morning in St Helena going round hotels and hairdressers' shops, but without success. She felt disheartened and tired, and she wondered what to do next. Several of the hotels had taken her name and said they would contact her if they needed someone, but she doubted whether she would ever hear anything.

She had lunch in one of the hotel restaurants, and had almost finished when she saw Jared coming in, his companion a beautiful blonde, her hair even whiter than Alice's own. Jealousy seared through her like a red-hot knife and she tried her hardest to ignore them, but time and time again her eyes turned in their direction, and suddenly Jared saw her.

His eyes widened in surprise and he immediately stood up and came over, excusing himself to his companion, who watched with interest.

'Alice, what are you doing here?' He slid into the empty seat opposite.

'What does it look like?' she shrugged.

'I mean—well, why? Why didn't you tell me you were coming in to St Helena? We could have eaten together.'

'I think your friend would have been disappointed.' Alice glanced across at the blonde, who was still watching them.

'Suzy?' Jared smiled warmly. 'Come and meet her. Bring your coffee. She's a nice girl, you'll like her.'

He picked her cup up, and Alice had no option but to follow.

'Suzy, I'd like you to meet Alice Alexander, the girl I told you about,' Jared introduced them.

Alice blinked. He had been talking about her?

'And Alice, this is Suzy. She's coming to dinner tonight.'

'I'm pleased to meet you, Alice,' said the girl, offering her hand.

Alice did her best to return her smile, shaking her hand and then sitting down, but Jared's news had devastated her. Suzy was coming to dinner! Why? Who was she? A new girlfriend? An old one? *Who?*

'You still haven't told me why you're here,' insisted Jared, and there was a slight frown on his brow.

Perhaps he thought it was something to do with Tony? 'Actually, I've been looking for a job,' she said. 'I feel lost now Luke's gone back to school.'

His brow cleared. 'Heavens, Alice! I could easily have——'

'No!' she interrupted. 'I wanted to find something myself.'

'And have you had any luck?'

She grimaced and shook her head. 'Though several people have taken my name and address.'

'I could help,' he said.

'No, thank you.'

'She's very independent,' Jared commented to Suzy with a smile.

'And why not?' said the girl. 'I'm all for it.'

'Shouldn't I have known I'd be outnumbered?' he groaned.

'We girls don't like to be beholden to anyone, isn't that right, Alice?' The blonde's unusual grey eyes were wide and frank as she looked across.

Alice nodded, wondering at the relationship between these two. It was so easy and lighthearted, yet the girl's eyes were on Jared often and it was obvious she was attracted. And what girl wouldn't be? she asked herself.

She finished her coffee. 'I think I'll go now, if you'll excuse me.'

But Jared would not hear of it. 'What's your rush?' Where are you going?' he asked.

'Home, I suppose,' she shrugged. 'I seem to have exhausted all the possibilities.'

'Then have another coffee and sit with us, and I'll take you myself.'

'But ——' Alice eyes rested on the other girl.

'Don't forget what we're supposed to be doing,' warned Suzy.

He nodded. 'At least let me find you a taxi, Alice.'

Alice wondered what Suzy's cryptic remark meant. What were they going to do? But she gave in. 'All right.' And she accepted another cup of coffee and sat and listened while they talked and ate. Suzy told him about her family, and it became clear that they had only just met. Love at first sight? wondered Alice, her insides going cold.

It was a relief when they had finished and they walked outside, and Jared hailed a taxi and put her in it paying the driver, directing him to Blue Vista.

'I'll see you later,' he said with a warm smile, but it was not enough to melt the ice that had formed round Alice's heart.

She nodded and he frowned, seeing the unhappiness in her eyes, but not guessing the reason for it. But it was too late for him to say anything, the driver was already pulling away.

When she got home and the afternoon stretched dauntingly ahead Alice began to wish she had stayed in St Helena. She wondered whether Tony was still there. His two weeks were up. Had he gone home? She had not seen him when she went to his hotel about a job, but that wasn't surprising, he could be on the beach or anywhere.

Her brow creased as she thought about him. He was definitely not the same person she had known in England, despite what Jared said about leopards never changing their spots. Or was it that she had not known him very well and he had now shown his true colours? She shrugged to herself. Who could say? But at least he hadn't carried out his threat and harmed Luke, for which she was thankful. Those last few days Luke was here had been very tense.

Eventually it was time to get showered and changed for dinner. Jared had not yet come home, but he never kept regular hours, so it didn't worry her. He would be here shortly, together with the beautiful Suzy. Alice was not looking forward to the evening.

She dressed carefully in a silky dress of summer blue. It dipped into a V at the front and the back, and she stroked the same colour shadow on to her eyelids and darkened her lashes with mascara. She piled her hair on top of her head with two glittering combs and pinned mother-of-pearl earrings on her ears.

But it was several minutes longer before she could school herself sufficiently to go downstairs. She had heard Jared moving about, and thought she heard Suzy's voice, and she did not want to join them, did not want to be an unwanted third party.

They were both on the terrace when she eventually sought them out, sipping champagne, Suzy already in a lighthearted mood. What were they celebrating? Alice wondered.

'Ah, Alice.' Jared rose courteously when he saw her.

'Hello,' she said softly. 'Hello, Suzy.' It was an effort to smile and she hoped the strain did not show.

'I was just telling Jared what a beautiful spot he has. I do envy you staying here.'

Jared guided Alice to her seat, filling her glass and handing the sparkling liquid to her.

'It is lovely, isn't it?' she agreed.

'Jared tells me it once belonged to your grandfather. Lucky you. Did you spend many holidays here?'

Alice flickered a glance at Jared. Exactly how much had he told this girl. 'No, I didn't. This is my first visit.'

'What a shame. Why was that? Did——'

'More champagne, Suzy?' Jared effectively silenced her, then steered the conversation into safer channels.

But as the evening progressed Alice could not help liking the other girl. She was open and friendly, and although it was clear she liked Jared a lot, she did not spend all her time talking to him and ignoring Alice. All in all it was quite a pleasant evening.

They ate their meal slowly, drank wine and coffee and brandy, and talked a lot, and laughed, then Jared played some of his classical tapes, and Alice was amazed when she saw it was after eleven.

'I think it's time I went to bed,' she said, stifling a yawn.

'And it's time I took you home, Suzy, if you're not to be late for work in the morning,' said Jared sternly.

She laughed into his face. 'You wouldn't be able to complain!'

Alice frowned. 'Does Suzy work for you, Jared?'

He turned to her and smiled. 'Yes. Didn't I tell you?'

He knew he hadn't, damn him. 'No, you didn't.'

'Typical!' scorned Suzy. 'I thought you knew. I've only just started, actually, and I love it already. Gosh, I bet you wanted to put a knife into my back!'

Alice's gaze shot from her to Jared then back again. 'Why would I feel that? Jared and I have nothing going.'

The girl flushed. 'But I thought—I understood, I——'

'You think too much,' laughed Jared. 'Come on, let's get you out of here before you put your foot into it altogether.'

'I'm sorry, Alice,' said Suzy, her hand to her mouth. 'I really am. That's my trouble, I always say what I'm thinking without stopping to wonder whether it's the right thing. I haven't embarrassed you?'

'Not at all.' Alice shook her head and smiled.

But when they had gone she began to wonder whether Suzy hadn't been relieved. It left her a clear field, and Jared did not seem to be uninterested. Considering Suzy had only just started working for his firm, they had a good relationship going. A bit like hers had been with him six years ago, lighthearted and carefree, where you could say what you thought and get away with it. But that was before she had fallen in love.

She lay in bed listening for Jared to return. He was a long time. A long, long time. Jealousy gnawed away inside her like a cancer. She tossed and turned, her ears alerted to the slightest sound, and it was after one when he finally returned.

What had they been doing for two hours? Alice's mind worked overtime. Talking? Kissing? Cuddling? Making love? It did not bear thinking about. She curled into the foetal position and screwed her eyes up tight and willed herself to go to sleep. But nothing happened. In the end she got up and went to the kitchen for a drink of milk, and after that she managed to get to sleep.

She woke late and the house was quiet; she guessed Jared had gone to work. It was Mrs Bell's day off as well, so she had the place to herself, and she wandered around in her nightie, munching a banana, drinking orange juice, and musing what to do with herself.

Jared came home at lunch time and she had only just got dressed. 'I've not cooked anything,' she said defensively. 'I wasn't expecting you.'

His brows rose at her tone. 'Would a salad and some of yesterday's cold chicken be too much trouble?' he enquired sardonically, selecting beer from the fridge and taking a long satisfying drink straight from the can.

Alice shrugged and began the preparations, and he swung round one of the kitchen chairs and straddled it, leaning his arms on the back, watching her.

'What do you think of Suzy?' he queried.

She flashed him a glance. 'She's all right.'

'She's a bright girl.'

'Good,' she said flatly.

'I think she'll do well.'

'What is she, your secretary?'

He laughed. 'Heavens, no! She's one of my agents. I'm taking her around and showing her what to do.'

In more ways than one, thought Alice viciously.

'What's the matter?' Jared caught her fleeting expression.

'Nothing.' She bent her head over the tomato she was slicing and did not see him get up.

The next moment his finger was under her chin, turning her face up to his. 'Jealous, Alice?'

'Why should I be?' she demanded, holding his gaze, feeling herself drowning in the depths of his blue eyes. How bright they were, how clear. How much they saw!

'You have no need to be,' he told her. 'Suzy is one of my employees, and that's all.'

Jared dropped his hand, but still she looked at him. 'You don't have to tell me,' she said.

'But I want you to know. I want you to be friends with her. I think she'd be good for you.'

'Really?' shrugged Alice

He nodded. 'Really. Once she's trained her hours will be irregular. You'll be able to go out together. I'm sure you'd like that, and she would too, she told me so.'

'If I get myself a job I'll make my own friends, thank you.'

He grimaced impatiently. 'Oh, Alice, why do you fight me so?'

'Because I don't like you organising my life,' she snapped.

'I'm not organising, I'm trying to help. You need a friend.'

'Someone who'll be able to report to you exactly where I've been, what I've been doing, and who with? No, thanks!' Alice renewed her attack on the tomatoes, throwing them on his plate and sending it skimming across the table towards him. 'Do you think I might try and see Tony, or something?'

Jared caught the plate just before it slid off the edge. 'Temper, temper, Alice!' he said warningly. 'And no, I don't think you'd be that foolish.' But his lips were grim and there was silence between them as they ate. She had angered him by bringing Tony's name into the conversation.

Suzy became a regular visitor, and Alice could not help but like her. The girl was good fun, her humour infectious, and the only thing that ruined it was Suzy's infatuation for Jared. He did not seem immune to her charms either, paying her more attention than Alice thought he should if she were a mere emloyee.

Suzy told Alice about her job, how it meant sitting around in the hotels and keeping her eyes open, discreetly checking on their security, seeing if any of the staff could be bribed, in general looking after the interests of the hotels that hired Jared.

It suddenly explained why he had been present in that hotel when Tony had accused him of spying, and Alice wished he had told her about his work. But he never did, and she had never liked to ask; she had always thought that if he wanted her to know he would tell her himself.

Alice tried the surrrounding towns for a job, but without success, and she became resigned to a long, boring holiday.

Then one weekend the phone rang, and it was the headmistress from Luke's school. Alice answered it, and Jared frowned as she handed him the receiver. 'I wonder what he's been doing?' he mouthed with a wry grimace, but his face grew serious as he listened. 'Of course, I'll come and fetch him. I'll come at once. Thank you for letting me know.'

Alice felt her heart miss a beat. 'What's happened?' she asked.

'He's broken his arm, would you believe.'

'Oh, no!' she cried, clapping her hands to her mouth.

'He's such a fearless little devil,' sighed Jared. 'He was climbing, hauling himself up somewhere, and fell.'

'And now he can't even use his crutches. Poor kid! Can I come with you?'

'I'll go alone,' he said. 'Just be waiting when I come back.'

'I will,' she whispered, and, leaning towards him, she kissed his cheek. It was the first time she had ever taken the initiative, and he looked at her in surprise, then he pulled her to him and kissed her mouth, and there was a whole depth of meaning in that brief kiss.

'Be waiting,' he repeated, when he put her from him, and his eyes were darker than normal, and he looked as through he would have liked to prolong their lovemaking.

The hours rolled slowly by. Luke's school was on St Lucia, so it meant a boat ride as well as the car journey, and Alice spent long minutes standing at the window, watching for Jared's car to appear.

When finally it came into sight she was outside and waiting before it stopped. Luke grinned at her as she opened his door, and he looked down at his plastered arm and the sling that was supporting it.

'What do you think you've been doing, young man?' she asked with mock severity.

'I was climbing a tree,' he said importantly.

'And how did you think you were going to manage that?'

He jutted his chin. 'I always do what the other boys do.'

He looked just like Jared at that moment, determined and aggressive, and oh, how she loved him!

Jared walked round the car, and Alice stepped back for him to lift Luke into his arms. She closed the car door and followed them into the house, and Jared deposited his son on the settee in the lounge.

'You do know what you've done, don't you?' she said to Luke, dropping to her knees in front of him. 'You've stopped yourself getting about. Wasn't it a stupid thing to do?'

Luke beamed. 'Tell her, Daddy.'

Jared smiled too. 'He has a wheelchair,' he told Alice.

'An electric one,' announced Luke importantly. 'I can work it with one hand. So you see I won't have to sit here all day.'

Alice looked questioningly at Jared. 'Is that right?' she

queried. He nodded. 'You bought it—today?'

'Heavens, no, he's had it for quite a while, but he's always scorned it,' said his father. 'The only problem is that the controls are on the right-hand side.'

And it was Luke's right arm he had broken! Alice looked at the little boy.

'I can still do it,' he said defiantly. 'Fetch it for me, Daddy.' Adding as an afterthought, 'Please.'

With a resigned shrug Jared left the room, and Alice sat beside Luke on the couch. 'Do you know what,' she said, 'I think you only did this so you'd be sent home.'

'No, I didn't,' he said indignantly. 'But I'm glad. I like it with you here, Alice. Will you play with me a lot now I'm hurt? Daddy said I'll need lots of attention.'

'Did he?' she laughed. 'I think he might have said you'll demand lots of attention.'

'What's demand?'

'Ask for, want, get everyone running around you.'

Luke nodded.

'But I don't think you'll be like that, will you, Luke? You'll still be able to do a lot of things.'

'Of course I will,' he said proudly. 'Ah, goody, here's my chair!'

Jared's eyes were twinkling as he lifted his son into the chair, and after a few scratches on the furniture, Luke managed to steer it reasonably well.

'Can I go outside, Daddy?' he asked.

Jared nodded. 'We'll come with you. But, Luke, remember this. You're never to go outside alone. I don't want you tipping yourself into the pool.'

And he didn't want to risk Tony being able to get his hands on him! Although they rarely mentioned Tony these days, Alice knew he was still very much in Jared's mind, especially now Luke was home.

Luke nodded. 'OK, Daddy. I could drown, couldn't I?

Because I can't swim with one arm.'

He was so grown-up sometimes. Alice exchanged a smile with Jared and they all three went out of the house. There were no steps, just a gentle slope, so it was a simple matter for Luke to manoeuvre himself. 'I had the ramp done when I bought the chair,' explained Jared.

They sat on the terrace watching Luke speed up and down, and round in circles. They drank iced lemon juice which Mrs Bell brought out to them, talking desultorily. But often they sat in companionable silence.

'I'm glad you're here,' said Jared.

Alice looked at him and smiled gently, feeling suddenly warm.

'For Luke's sake. He'll need some company. It's difficult for me to get time off at the moment.'

Disappointment welled inside her, but she should have known it wasn't anything personal. It was only fleetingly that he ever showed any true warmth, and when he did he would back off so quickly that she sometimes wondered whether he regretted it. She could not understand him.

'And he'll need watching,' he added warningly.

Alice swallowed hard. 'I know.' And there was no need for him to say any more.

The next day, which was Monday, Jared went to work, and that evening Suzy came to dinner. Luke was allowed to stay up late as a special treat, but he was strangely subdued, and Suzy did not seem to know how to treat him. She looked uncomfortable, which was unlike her and when Luke said he wanted to go to bed Alice offered to take him.

'I don't like her,' he said, once they were in his room. 'She keeps looking at me.'

'That's because you're a lovely little boy.'

'I'm not little!' he declared angrily.

'OK, you're a big boy. Actually I don't think Suzy's

ever had anything to do with children like you. You mustn't mind. She'll soon get used to you.' Alice had learned in the early days that Luke did not mind her talking about his disability. It did not seem to worry him that he was different—in fact he seemed quite proud of it.

'Does she come here a lot?' he frowned.

'Quite a lot.'

'Daddy says she works for him.'

'That's right.'

'He's never brought anybody here from work before.'

Alice smiled. 'He thought she'd be company for me.'

'Oh,' he said, then his eyelids began to droop and in seconds he was asleep.

Alice rejoined Jared and Suzy, and they sat outside in the warm dusky air and Alice wished it were just the two of them. Why did he keep bringing this other girl? She enjoyed Suzy's company, but she did not need her, especially now Luke was here. Was it that Jared fancied her himself?

In the days that followed Alice spent all of her time with Luke, but Suzy was still a constant visitor, gradually learning to relax with the small boy. He was full of mischief, his broken arm not bothering him one little bit.

Alice thought he too was growing fond of Suzy until one day he said, 'I wish Suzy didn't come here. Why does she?'

'Because your daddy asks her,' she said, tucking him into bed, wishing the same thing herself.

'Do you think Daddy loves Suzy? Do you think he's going to marry her?'

Alice lifted her shoulders, trying to hide the pain his questions caused. 'That's something you'll have to ask him yourself.'

'I hope he doesn't, I don't want him to. I want him to marry you, Alice. I love you.'

'And I love you,' she whispered, hugging him.

'I want you to stay here for always.'

'I can't do that,' she told him.

'Why?'

'Because this isn't my house. It's yours and your daddy's. I'm only here because of my grandfather's will.'

'If you married my daddy you could stay here.'

Alice pulled a wry face. 'I don't think I shall do that.'

'Why, don't you love him?'

'Luke, there's no point in me loving your father when he doesn't love me,' she said gently.

'How do you know he doesn't love you? I think he does.'

'Mr Know-It-All, are you?' she teased. 'And what makes you think that?'

'Because he keeps looking at you,' Luke answered simply, 'and he has a silly look on his face—I've seen it on television. He does love you, Alice. He doesn't look at Suzy the same way.'

'And yet a minute ago you asked me if he was going to marry Suzy! I think you're having me on Luke. Close your eyes now and go to sleep.' Alice kissed his cheek and left the room, but his comments set her mind working.

He must be wrong, though. She had never seen Jared looking at her with anything remotely like love in his eyes. Luke was imagining it. It was wishful thinking because he wanted her to be his mummy.

After a few days Luke became bored staying around the house. 'Can't you take me out, Alice?' he begged. 'In Daddy's car?'

Alice had thought Jared would object, but he surprised her by agreeing. 'I don't see why not,' he said, and as he always used his battered sports car for work, declaring it gave him anonymity when he was touring the hotels, she had the pleasure of driving his opulent saloon.

Luke sat in the front seat, beaming happily, and in St

Helena they stopped for an ice-cream. Then they went on along the coast until they came to the restaurant near the beach where Jared had taken Alice the first week she was here.

Alice parked the car, and it was a struggle, but she managed to get Luke into his chair, and from then on he was free, riding round the tables, laughing aloud with the sheer joy of being somewhere different. There were several other diners and they all smiled at the small boy in his wheelchair.

They ate their lunch, and gradually the tables emptied until there was only themselves left. 'I think we should be going,' said Alice, 'but first I have to go to the ladies' room. Will you be all right? I'll only be a moment.' There were steps into the building, so she could not take Luke with her. Earlier, when Luke had wanted to go to the toilet himself, she had enlisted the help of one of the hotel staff to carry him inside.

Luke nodded. 'Of course.'

'Now don't go wandering off,' she admonished, knowing what he was like. He only had to see something and he was wheeling away to take a closer look. His once-scorned wheelchair had given him a new kind of freedom. He could get about much faster than on his crutches and he was an inquisitive little boy.

'I promise,' he said.

Alice was no more than a couple of minutes, but when she got outside Luke had gone. His chair was there, but the child himself had disappeared.

Panic hit her. Tony! It was Tony. All this time he had been waiting his chance, and she had given it to him without even thinking. There hadn't been a soul about. She hadn't even thought about Tony. And now he had struck. Oh God what was she going to do? What was Jared going to say? She raced around questioning the staff, looking here and there and everywhere, even though it was pointless. Luke wasn't here. He was gone. He had been kidnapped!

Her heart was cold with dread as she used the restaurant's telephone to ring Jared.

# CHAPTER TEN

'WHAT do you mean, Luke's disappeared?' Jared's voice jarred in Alice's ear.

'I only popped to the ladies' and when I came out his chair was empty. I've searched everywhere, Jared!' There was a break in her voice.

He was silent for a moment, a long empty silence when she knew he was blaming her. Then he said, 'Are you sure you've looked everywhere? You know what he's like, he could have got someone to lift him out of his chair just for fun, to frighten you.'

'I have looked, all the staff have looked. He's not here, Jared.'

'Have you informed the police?' he asked tersely.

'No, I thought I should tell you first.'

'Yes, of course. I'm on my way.'

The line went dead, and Alice replaced the receiver and returned to Luke's wheelchair. She looked at it intently, as if she could will him to return. Oh, Tony, Tony, why have you done this? she cried silently. Why? Why does money mean so much to you?

She walked up and down, half out of her mind with worry, not listening when the restaurant manager bade her sit down. How could she sit still when Luke was missing and it was all her fault?

When Jared arrived she ran to him. His face was grim, his eyes hard as he looked at her. 'Can't I trust you, Alice? Can't I trust you to look after Luke? Why did you leave him? Why did you take your eyes off him? You know as

173

well as I do that his life was in danger.'

'Jared, please!' Alice recoiled under the hardness in his tone. 'There was no one about. I never dreamt—I never dreamt for one minute that Tony would carry out his threat. It's been so long, I thought——'

He cut her short with an imperative sweep of his hand. 'Luke's the only person in this world I care about. Without him my life is meaningless.'

'I know,' she whispered painfully.

'Tell me again exactly what happened,' he ordered.

While she related the events Jared listened, tight-lipped, then he searched the restaurant and surrounding area himself. 'There's a chance,' he said, 'a slim chance, that it's all some huge practical joke on Luke's part. He went missing once before and I called in the police, and he was found hiding in a cave in the mountain, highly delighted by all the trouble he'd caused. Needless to say he was severely chastised.'

'And you think he might have done this again?' Alice clutched at the straw he had offered her.

'If he could get someone to help him. But don't forget he's not on his crutches. I think we should go home and think this out.'

'You're not calling the police?'

'Not yet.'

'I think you should,' she said.

'Well, I don't!' snarled Jared, and his tone brooked no argument.

And so they went—in separate cars. And at Blue Vista they found it—the ransom note. The sum of money being asked for made Alice's eyes widen. She could not believe Tony was so greedy.

Jared's face was grey and grim as he poured himself a Scotch, pacing the house, not speaking to Alice, and she knew he blamed her. But it was not fair. How could it be her fault? Who would have dreamt that Tony would act so swiftly? He must have been watching her all the time. Her skin crawled at the thought.

Then the phone rang and Jared answered it, his lips tightening as he listened to whoever was on the other end. 'That was Suzy,' he said, when he finally replaced the receiver. 'She's been watching Tony for me. When you said Luke was missing I thought he must have given her the slip. But it wasn't him. He left the island early this morning and boarded a flight to England from St Lucia several hours ago.'

'I see,' said Alice quietly. It was good news and yet it wasn't. She was glad Tony wasn't involved, but if he hadn't got Luke then who had? The whole affair suddenly grew more serious. Tony wouldn't have harmed Luke, she felt sure. He might have tried to frighten Jared, but that was all. But now, whoever had the boy could be in deadly earnest.

'Is there someone else who has it in for you?' she asked quietly. 'Someone who wants to hurt you through Luke?'

Jared shook his head. 'No one that I can think of.'

He looked a broken man, his head bent, his shoulders bowed, and she went up to him and touched his arm, not caring that he was blaming her, wanting only to comfort him.

'Jared, I'm sure it will be all right. I'm sure whoever's got Luke won't hurt him.'

He did not answer.

'He can't be far away, can he? The island's not all that big.'

He flashed her a scathing glance. 'Have you any idea what it will be like for him? It's bad enough that he can't walk, but with a broken arm as well he's completely in their hands.'

'Luke's a brave boy. He's probably enjoying it.'

'Enjoying it?' he snarled, jumping to his feet. 'What a stupid thing to say! He's probably scared out of his wits. I wish there was something I could do. I wish——'

The telephone rang again and he hurled himself across the room, grabbing the receiver and barking his name into it.

Alice watched his face for telltale signs.

'Where . . .? Yes . . . *No . . .!* I haven't got that much right here. I'll have to get it . . . I want to speak to Luke . . . *Yes, now, dammit!* Luke, son, how are you . . .? Where are you . . . *What . . .?* God, you're crazy. Yes, she's here . . . I'll tell her . . . Luke, you must tell me where you are . . . *Luke?'* He crashed the phone down. 'He's gone.'

Alice gripped Jared's arms. 'What did they say? What did Luke say? Is he all right?'

'Luke's fine,' he said hoarsely. 'Just fine.' He shook his head in disbelief. 'You were right, he thinks it's some huge game. He says to tell you he was sorry he couldn't wait.'

Alice closed her eyes and groaned, burying her face in Jared's chest.

His arms came around her and he held her to him. 'He doesn't know where he is, of course, and he says he's had plenty to eat, but that he's tired now and he's going to sleep.'

'Didn't he give you any idea at all where he was?' she asked.

Jared shook his head. 'In a big house, but he'd obviously said too much, because the line went dead the minute he said it.'

Alice lifted her face to look at him, her eyes moist, her face pale. 'What are we going to do?' she asked faintly.

'There's not much we can do at the moment. I'll get the money together and——'

'*No!* Jared, no—you can't! It's too much, even if you've got that sort of money.'

'You think Luke's not worth it?' he rasped, letting her go again and staring at her as though she were out of her mind.

'Oh, God, of course not, Jared. I love him as much as you do. But I think you ought to call the police now. It's too much for you to handle.'

'Don't forget I was once in the police force myself. I know a thing or two. In fact——' He stopped abruptly, looking at her and yet not seeing her. 'Alice—I've got it! I think I know where he might be.'

'You do?' Her eyes widened.

'Yes. Luke didn't say *a* big house. He said *the* big house. That's got to be it! I know where he means. What a clever lad he is! He told me. He told me, Alice!'

For the first time in hours Jared smiled, and he grabbed Alice and kissed her, and despite the circumstances she could not help feeling a surge of warmth, a tingling through her limbs, and she kissed him back, putting every ounce of feeling into that kiss.

He withdrew a few inches and looked at her, frowning, then he groaned and kissed her again, his passion matching her own. 'I love you, Alice,' he mouthed, then he let her go and was hurrying across the room.

Still reeling from the shock of what he had said, Alice could only watch. At the door he turned. 'I shouldn't be long.'

'Jared, wait! Where are you going? *Jared!*'

But he had gone.

Alice clapped her hands to her face and just stood there. Jared loved her. *He loved her!* She couldn't believe it. She didn't believe it. He hadn't known what he was saying. He was out of his mind with worry about Luke and had spoken without thinking.

Then she suddenly realised he was going alone to this place where he thought Luke was. He could be in danger.

She ran after him, but his ancient sports car was already pulling out of the drive.

Slowly she walked back into the house, but she could not relax and she wished there was something she could do.

Mrs Bell was equally concerned when Alice told her Jared had gone off alone to tackle the kidnappers. 'Mercy me, he might get himself killed!' she exclaimed.

That was what Alice thought too, and she had never known time go so slowly. She went up to Luke's room and looked at his toys and the empty bed, and tears filled her eyes. 'Please God, don't let him get hurt. Let him be all right,' she whispered.

She went into Jared's bedroom too. It was the first time she had ever been in there. It was neat and spartan—a man's room. No fuss or trimmings. A plain bedcover, a plain tiled floor; a wardrobe and a set of drawers, a chair and a full-length mirror, and that was all. There were no socks lying on the floor, or a shirt on the back of the chair. It did not look lived in. It needed a woman's touch.

Back downstairs, Alice was drawn to the photographs, and she picked up one of Jared and studied it intently. Not that she needed to. His image was imprinted in her memory for all time. If she never saw him again she would always remember what he looked like.

And there was Luke, grinning mischievously. Come back safely, she prayed. You and your daddy. I love you both.

And Jared loved her!

It was a wonderfully exciting thought and she hoped it was true. They ought to be here by now. She went to the window and looked out, and Mrs Bell joined her, but the minutes ticked away and there was no sign of them.

'What do you think's happened?' Alice asked the housekeeper, nearly in tears.

The woman shrugged her ample shoulders. 'Don't ask me, missy. I have no idea.'

Jared was hurt. He had marched in and the kidnappers had shot him. He was dead. Luke too. All sorts of thoughts chased through Alice's half-crazed mind. She thought of ringing the police, but what could she tell them? She had no idea where Jared had gone. The big house—which house? It could be any house. It meant something to Jared and to Luke, but not to anyone else. Oh Lord, where were they?

The shrill ring of the telephone burst into the silence and made her jump. She looked at Mrs Bell and the woman looked at her, and Alice was afraid to answer it. It was probably the police telling her there had been an accident and Jared was dead. Some accident! Oh God, why hadn't she kept a closer eye on Luke? It was all her fault. It was——

'Shouldn't you be answering that, missy?'

Alice pulled herself together and picked up the phone, putting it gingerly to her ear, not really wanting to hear what she was going to be told.

'Alice?' It was Luke's voice.

'Oh, Luke!' Tears rolled down her cheeks. 'Oh, Luke, baby! Are you all right?'

'Course I'm all right,' he said impatiently. 'Alice, are you crying?'

'No,' she sniffed. 'Where are you? Are you coming home?'

'Daddy wants a word with you.'

Jared spoke into the phone almost immediately. 'Alice, can you come and fetch us?'

She felt shocked. 'Yes, but why? What's happened? Are you hurt? Can't you drive? Jared, what's wrong?'

'This is no time for questions,' he rasped. 'Turn left out of the gates and follow the road up the mountain.'

'Up?' she queried. Where did that lead to? She had never been there.

'Yes, that's right, up. After about a mile and a half you'll see a shoot-off to your right, take that and follow it for a further half mile. The house is in the trees. There's no one else here, so you needn't worry.'

'But, Jared——'

'Have you got that?' he demanded.

'Yes.'

'Then get going!'

'Yes, Jared, I'm coming now. I'll be with you as soon as I can.'

It was almost dark as Alice headed the car out of the drive. The headlights cut a tunnel of light into the gloom, but even so she almost missed the turning. It was just a track, uneven and narrow, and she could still not imagine why Jared had asked her to fetch them. Had he smashed his car? She wished he had told her.

Where was the house? She slowed even more, her eyes searching the blackness, and then she saw it gleaming white through the trees. It *was* a big house—enormous. She drove up to it and got out, but she left the lights on and the engine running.

The front door was closed, but Jared had said there was no one else here, so she pushed it open and stepped inside. 'Jared? Luke?' she called.

No one answered.

She felt like screaming. Was this a trap? Was she going to be held prisoner too? All sorts of wild thoughts raced through her head, and she wondered whether she ought to get out while she could and fetch the police.

But no. She trusted Jared. He wouldn't have led her into danger. *'Jared!'* This time she yelled at the top of her voice. *'Luke!* Where are you?'

When Jared stepped out of the darkness she jumped in alarm, then rushed to him impulsively and threw herself into his arms. 'Oh, Jared, are you all right?' she gasped.

'Yes, Alice.' He held her tightly, as though he needed her too.

'I was so worried, desperately worried. What happened? Where's Luke? Is he all right? Oh, Jared, I was so afraid for you!' She turned her face up to his, looking at him in the light from the car's headlamps.

'You sound as though you mean it,' he observed.

'I do. If anything had happened to you I would have wanted to die!'

'I'm flattered,' he said drily.

'This whole mess is my fault.'

'And you couldn't stand the guilt? I see.' He released her abruptly. 'Let's go and get Luke.' He did not give her the chance to deny it.

'What happened?' she asked, hurrying after him. 'Where are the kidnappers?'

'Gone,' he said shortly.

'You didn't—Jared, you didn't give them the money?'

'No,' he thrust over his shoulder.

'I don't understand,' she insisted.

'We'll talk later. Our first priority is getting Luke home.'

'Of course,' she said.

Luke was asleep, curled on a sofa with a blanket over him. A candle flickered in the room, but that was the only form of light. Jared lifted him and he stirred but he did not wake as Jared carried him out to the car.

Alice sat in the back with Luke's head on her lap, and the journey down the mountain was made in silence. She was desperate to question him, but Jared seemed in no mood to talk.

Luke woke when Jared began to undress him, and he smiled wanly at Alice, but he was still drugged with sleep, and the moment he was into his pyjamas and tucked into bed, he went to sleep again. He looked so pale and tired that her heart went out to him. What an ordeal for such a young child!

Back downstairs Jared poured himself a Scotch, took a long much-needed swallow and then dropped into an armchair, his legs stretched out in front of him, his head back, his eyes closed.

Alice sat too, watching him, and after a few moments he opened his eyes and smiled ruefully. 'What a day!'

'And it was all my fault.'

'No,' he said quietly. 'I know I said that in the heat of the moment, but it could have happened at any time. You were in no way to blame.'

'I still feel guilty, whether you blame me or not,' she said. 'Who did it, Jared, and why? Have you any idea?'

He nodded. 'Oh, yes, I know who did it. It was someone I once sent to prison.'

Alice's eyes widened. 'I see. Has he just come out or something?'

'Good God, no! He's been out years. A reformed character, so I understood. Opened his own restaurant, though it always puzzled me where he got the money. He said he inherited it, but I wouldn't mind betting it was an accumulation from his crimes.'

'But why would he suddenly decide to take his revenge, after all this time? Especially if he's now running a successful business.'

'Successful but not entirely legitimate, and it was Suzy who stumbled on it.'

Aliced frowned.

'She's really keen on this security game, and it's become second nature to her to look over any restaurant or hotel that she goes to,' Jared explained. 'And she found one hell of a fiddle going on. She reported it to the proprietor, thinking she was doing him a favour, and he was so adamant that she was wrong that she thought he must be trying to hide something.

'She told me about it and I advised her to report it to the police, and it was ultimately discovered that the restaurant was a cover-up for much shadier dealings. Our good friend's still free at the moment—he's out on bail, I believe —but it won't be long before he's behind bars again—for a very long time.'

'And because Suzy works for you he thought you were behind it all and decided to get his own back by kidnapping Luke? So what happened? Where is he now?'

'He didn't do the job himself, Alice, it was two of his cronies. I think I put the fear of God into them. When I got there I fused the lights and took them by surprise.' Jared grinned. 'My martial arts training came in pretty useful as well! They didn't stand a chance.'

'But you let them go instead of turning them over to the police?'

He laughed. 'They couldn't wait to get out of there! They weren't really criminals, just a couple of guys whom my old friend had bribed into doing his dirty work for him.'

'They took your car?' she asked.

'They thought it would stop me following them. They didn't realise that with one phone call I could have the road blocked and they would never have got away.'

'Aren't you worried he might try it again?'

'He won't. His case comes up next week.'

'Who does the house belong to?' Alice asked.

'A friend of mine,' said Jared. 'She's in Europe at the moment. It's common knowledge that the house is empty for three months of every year. Won't she be surprised when I tell her what's been going on!'

'A close friend of yours?' Alice queried.

He looked at her intently. 'Jealous, Alice?'

'I know I shouldn't be, but I am,' she admitted.

'And why shouldn't you be?'

'Because what you do with your life is nothing to do

with me.'

'But what you do with your life means a lot to me,' Jared said quietly.

She frowned. 'Because of my grandfather?'

He sat up straight. 'Alice, come here,' he ordered.

Hesitantly she got up and moved towards him, stopping when she was a few inches away, and looking down, her eyes puzzled.

'Tell me, Alice, were you really as concerned for my safety as you made out?'

Her reply was instantaneous. 'Of course I was!'

'And did you mean that about wanting to die too if anything happened to me?'

She nodded.

'Not simply because you felt guilty?'

'No.' Her voice was barely audible now.

'Then why?'

'Isn't it obvious?' she asked. Why was he putting her through this cross-examination?

'Could it be that you—love me, Alice? That you still love me? That you've never stopped loving me?'

She closed her eyes. 'Don't make me say it!' she whispered.

She felt him take her hands. 'Is it such a hard thing to say, Alice? You didn't think so six years ago.'

'I let my heart rule my head then.'

'But now it's the other way round?'

She nodded.

'Alice, look at me.' Reluctantly she lifted her lids. 'I said something to you, Alice, when I went out after Luke. Did you hear what I said?'

'Yes,' she whispered.

'You didn't think I meant it?'

She pulled a wry face. 'I hoped you did, but I thought you were too worried about Luke to know what you were saying.'

'I did mean it, Alice. I've wanted to tell you for so long, but there's always been Tony. I've never known quite what your feelings for him were.'

'I don't love him,' she said strongly. 'I never have. I don't think I even like him any more. He wasn't the person I thought.'

'You're sure?' Jared insisted.

'I'm sure,' agreed Alice.

He grinned and pulled her down on to his lap. 'So, Alice, tell me what I want to hear.'

This time there was no holding back. 'I love you, Jared.' She looked into the deep blue of his eyes and saw them darken with desire. She stroked back the hair at his temples. 'I love you very much.' She felt him tremble. 'I've never stopped loving you. But I truly never thought this day would come.'

'Nor me,' he muttered, curving a palm behind her head and urging her face towards his. 'Nor me, Alice.'

His kiss was deep and long and drugging. Time was forgotten, nothing mattered except the importance of this moment. This was a bonding of their love, a silent commitment.

'I wonder how long it would have taken us if Luke hadn't been kidnapped?' Jared asked, breaking off finally to just look at her. His fingers explored her face, her eyelids and brows, her cheekbones, the contours of her nose, the outline of her lips.

Alice touched his fingertips with her tongue and heard his indrawn breath. 'I guess for ever,' she said. 'I was convinced you didn't love me, that you were only putting up with me for Daniel's sake.'

'And I was convinced you didn't love me. I know you responded to me physically, but hell, I wanted more than that!'

She touched his lips now, and he caught her fingers and kissed them and pressed her palm to his cheek, and all his love for her shone in his eyes. 'When did you discover you loved me, Jared?'

'I think I loved you a little bit when you were sweet sixteen. But I was married, and my marriage vows meant a lot to me. I was totally shocked when you declared you loved me. You've no idea how I felt!'

'You were angry,' she protested.

'I had to be, my darling. It was the only way.'

'Did you ever tell my grandfather how you felt?'

Jared shook his head. 'But he probably guessed. I mentioned you so often he must have done.'

'If I'd never come here would you have come to England again?'

'Yes, Alice, I would have done. It had been in my mind for a long time. But I couldn't be sure that I wouldn't be making a fool of myself. I was convinced that on your part it was infatuation.'

'And now you know differently.'

He nodded. 'I want you with me for always, Alice. I want us to get married.'

'I want that too,' she breathed in his ear, nibbling it, teasing him with her tongue, so that he turned his head round and claimed her mouth.

'I'm glad you love Luke as well,' he said at length.

'I guess you wouldn't have asked me to marry you if I didn't?'

'It was important to me,' he admitted. 'I wonder whether Luke will approve of you as his new mother?'

Alice's lips twisted in amusement. 'He's already told me he'd like me to fill that position,' she announced primly. 'Not Suzy. He doesn't like her so much.'

'Oh, he has, has he? The little devil! I never realised his mind worked that way. I must tell him I prefer to choose my own wife.'

'You haven't had an affair with Suzy, have you?' she asked quietly. 'Only sometimes when you take her home you're away for a long time.'

'Purely business talk, my jealous little future wife. I wanted her to be your friend, that's all. I thought you needed someone.'

'I needed you,' she assured him.

'And God, how I needed you!' Jared groaned, and kissed her again, and this time the kiss went on and on, and his hand slid inside her blouse to cup her breast, sending fresh shivers of delight through her body.

She arched herself against him, and finally he carried her up to his bedroom, where they made love. It was all and more than Alice had dreamt of. It was magical, exciting, mind-blowingly beautiful.

And in the morning they both went to see Luke and tell him the good news.

He took it very matter-of-factly, as though it had been merely a matter of course. 'Oh, good,' he said, then went on to tell Alice about the kidnappers.

He was full of it for days afterwards, but at least it kept him happy while the arrangements for the wedding were taking place.

And a week later a letter was delivered to Alice from Tony. A letter which obliterated the last trace of regret from her mind.

> Dear Alice,
> What an idiot I was. I let my obsession for money blind me to everything else. We'd always been poor and I'd had enough of seeing my parents struggle to make ends meet. Although I'm lucky in that I have a good job I always promised myself I'd marry someone rich, so it seemed like my dream could come true when your grandfather died and left you his money. I was already

fond of you, Alice, and I thought that was enough. I think you liked me a little bit too, until I overstepped the mark. I would never have harmed Luke, I promise you that. He's a nice kid, and Jared isn't bad too. I hope it works out for you. It's taken me a while to come to my senses, but I've at last realised that money doesn't buy happiness.

With deepest apologies,

Tony.

'Jared,' said Alice softly.

'Mmm?'

'I have something to tell you.'

'Oh, yes? I don't think I can stand to hear yet again that you love me.'

'Beast!'

They were lying out in the sun by the pool. They had been married six weeks, and Alice was blissfully happy.

'I think Luke's going to have a brother.'

Silence for a second or two, then Jared sprang to his feet. 'What? Already? You don't mean it?'

She nodded.

'Have you been to see a doctor?'

'No, but I know, believe me.' She patted her perfectly flat tummy. 'He's in here, and he's going to look just like you.'

His face softened and he touched her reverently. 'I think it might be a girl. Luke would like a sister.'

'It might be twins.'

His eyes widened. 'Is there that possibility?'

She shrugged. 'I don't think so, unless there are twins on your side. But it would be nice.'

'I have a surprise for you too,' he grinned. 'Stay there and I'll bring it out.'

He disappeared into the house, and Alice could not

imagine what it was. Another necklace? More perfume? He had showered her with gifts, but his love was more precious than anything money could buy, and she never failed to tell him so. It still felt like a miracle that he loved her, and she prayed that nothing would ever happen to ruin her happiness.

When Luke returned he had a stiff cream envelope in his hand. He handed it to her with a smile. 'Mr Lewis entrusted me with the honour,' he explained.

Alice frowned. 'What is it?'

'How long have you been here, Alice?'

She thought a moment, then her eyes widened. 'Three months! Have I really been here that long? I can't believe it.'

'That's because you're married to me and I make you supremely happy.'

Alice put her tongue out.

'Aren't you going to open it?' asked Jared.

'It doesn't really matter now, does it?' she taunted. 'I found another way of getting rich.'

'Bitch!' he mouthed, sliding on to the sun-lounger beside her. 'I always wondered why you married me. I think you deserve to be punished for that.' His mouth claimed hers and the kiss was feverish and uncontrollable and she loved it, and if there hadn't been the danger of Luke or Mrs Bell coming out and seeing them they would have made love there and then. She could not get enough of Jared, nor he of her, and they had talked about getting rid of the housekeeper, so that when Luke was at school they could make love where and whenever they liked.

He picked up the envelope and waved it yet again before her eyes. 'Come on, I'm as impatient as you to see what Dan's left you.'

'You don't know?'

He shook his head. 'No.'

With an impish smile Alice sat up and turned her back to him, slitting the envelope open with her thumb and sliding out the single sheet of paper. She felt Jared looking over her shoulder and turned away so that he should not yet see, then as she finished reading she became convulsed with laughter.

'What's the matter?' Jared was laughing too. 'Come on, let me see it.'

'What a man!' she said, and raising her eyes to the heavens she said, 'If you're up there, Grandfather, thank you. Thank you from the bottom of my heart.'

'I wish I knew what you were talking about,' grumbled Jared goodnaturedly. 'What's he left you? You certainly look happy enough.'

'Nothing,' she said. 'Sweet Fanny Adams.'

He frowned. 'Then why were you thanking him?'

'Because he left me—here, read it for yourself.' She held the letter so that they could read it together.

My dearest Alice,

The news of your mother's death was a deep shock to me, and I know I shall not live many more days. I love you, even though I've never met you. Jared has told me a lot about you, and I think he loves you too, although he never said as much to me. You were just a child and he was married, and he's a very honourable man.

They looked at each other and smiled. 'Are you honourable?' Alice asked Jared wickedly.

I wish I had something to leave you. You'll have learned by now of the misfortune I had. Blue Vista was my home and I loved it. It broke my heart to sell, but Jared let me carry on living here as though it were still my own. He treated me like the family I never had. Don't feel too badly when I say this. It wasn't your fault.

I hope that now your three months is over you've learned to love Blue Vista and the island as much as I did, but I hope more than that, more than anything, that you've learned to love Jared. He was all I had, he meant more to me than anyone else, and he is what I leave to you, my dearest, dearest Alice.

'My God!' said Jared.

Alice grinned.

You probably think this is a strange inheritance, but I know Jared loves you, and he hinted that you were fond of him, so I hope that by now your love has grown and that you will make my dreams come true and marry him. It is my one last wish. None of my others have come true.

I know I won't be there to see whether it does, but I have a feeling in my bones that it will, and I'm happier at this moment, now I've written to you, than I have been in a long time.

All my love, Alice, and God bless.

Daniel.

There were tears in her eyes as she finished. Jared's eyes looked suspiciously moist too.

'What a crafty old bastard,' he said.

'He deliberately threw us together.'

'He knew what would happen.'

'I think I love him,' said Alice.

Jared caught her face between his hands. 'That, my darling, is the nicest thing you could possibly say.'